CW01648581

# The Perils of Discovering Time Travel

## -The Rescue of Travis Calder

(Story 1 Book 1)

J. S. Leon

This book is dedicated to my buddy's son, Ollie McCutcheon, who inspired the concept...it's proof that the wonders of children can motivate the thoughts and ideas of men.

Much love little man!

Table of Contents:

## Chapter 1: The Prize

**Microsoft Imagine Cup/LSU Campus…May 17th, 2027**

The atrium of the Louisiana State University's science building buzzed like a beehive, each booth its own hive cell, humming with frantic voices, last-minute adjustments, and the smell of soldering irons. Hand-painted posters sagged on pushpins. Model volcanoes still smoked faintly from vinegar eruptions. A homemade drone whined above the crowd; dodging balloons tied to folding chairs. The competition was well underway. The Microsoft Imagine Cup where the best and the brightest in the nation competed with their scientific submissions. Usually, the yearlong contest concluded at the Microsoft building, but this year was different. In an attempt to garner more interest, Microsoft announced they would be holding their future competitions on college campuses across the country. Anna Ruiz, a journalism major, had submitted the essay that won LSU the honor of being the first chosen destination off site.

Travis Calder, an exceptionally brilliant student with the registered I.Q. to prove it, adjusted his tie for the third time. Although he always dressed in a preppy style he hated ties. They made him feel like he was choking. But his roommate insisted that "first impressions win prizes." Travis knew that the torturous accessory was unnecessary. Still, here he was, wearing the tie, sweat prickling under his collar, standing next to a black velvet-lined display case and a device that, if he was right, would change history, making this stupid tie completely useless. He surveyed the competition from his post realizing he was nervous for no reason. He knew what he had was miles ahead of his peers.

"Quantum Vision Goggles," read the neat white placard.

They didn't look like much—bulky black frames, thicker than ski goggles, a faint shimmer running through the lenses as though oil floated inside the glass. A small dial protruded from the right earpiece, a silver button gleamed on the left, and a tiny speaker was affixed to each earpiece. It was clumsy. Unpolished. But they worked. For public display purposes, they had a wire attaching them to a big screen television allowing those in attendance to view everything he was seeing through the goggles in real time. When Travis slid them over his eyes and twisted the dial, the universe bent. The space in front of him shimmered through the goggles as light seemed to bend around air itself and then suddenly, he was looking at the past through the eyes of someone that was never even there.

He exhaled slowly, steadying his hands.

As he looked around, the television projected a scene of what he was seeing.

And what he saw around him was much different than what the other spectators were witnessing.

People began to notice.

The judges approached like a stormfront. Three professors, two donors in tailored suits, and one skeptical-looking graduate student, who carried a clipboard like a weapon.

Travis cleared his throat.

"Ladies and gentlemen, what you're seeing is not a simulation. Not a recording. It is reality, refracted through time itself."

They shifted impatiently.

He lifted the glasses, careful, reverent, as if unveiling an artifact. He placed them on his face and turned the dial three clicks back. The shimmer deepened.

The atrium dissolved. Deeper into its own history.

Before him, the same room appeared—but younger. Bright banners reading WELCOME, CLASS OF 1973! hung crookedly from the rafters. Bell-bottomed students mingled. A hippie junior strummed a guitar in the corner as he attempted to perform his all-original folk songs. A janitor mopped near where Travis's own booth now stood. The sound was faint, like a radio playing far away, but it was there: laughter, chatter, music.

The judges gasped. One of the donors muttered, "Is this... a recording?"

The oldest of the judges stepped forward. He had been part of the graduating class of 1974, in charge of welcoming new freshmen as part of his duties in student council all but his own freshman year of college.

He studied the scene on the television. Familiar but confusing. All of a sudden, he turned white as a ghost, there he was. His younger self anyways. All he could do was stare at the monitor with a dropped jaw as his younger version walked right into frame and reached out to shake the hand of a nervous underclassman.

"How did you get this young man? I don't remember the event being recorded."

Travis twisted the dial forward. The haze shifted. The banners vanished. The atrium stood empty, sunlight streaking through dust. He pushed the button on the left side earpiece and the vision snapped back to now—judges blinking, crowd rustling, the drone buzzing overhead.

"No recording," Travis said softly. "This is the actual past of this room, viewed through quantum refractive lens. The glasses allow the user to dial in a date and time—any date, any time—from the past, and witness exactly what occurred in the space around them at that precise moment. It continues to play out the events until you press stop."

For what seemed like several minutes, waves of whispers. Then the atrium erupted.

Students swarmed forward, straining to see. Judges whispered in astonishment. The grad student scribbled furiously. Someone demanded, "Show us something from yesterday!" Another shouted, "Last week's basketball game!"

Travis adjusted the dial again—February 18th, 11:45 p.m. The atrium shimmered. Empty, save for a lone janitor sweeping, humming a cheerful tune. Stop. Back 2 more hours, just in time to see the winning shot at the buzzer of last week's basketball game as requested. Stop. Back to present.

Gasps again.

The donors exchanged glances, money in their eyes.

The head judge—a stern woman with iron-gray hair—stepped forward.

"Mr. Calder... are you suggesting you have built a window into history?"

Travis swallowed, his throat dry. "Yes, ma'am. A window you can wear."

The applause was thunderous.

The award ceremony blurred together after that. His name echoing across the atrium. A gleaming plaque placed in his hands. Cameras flashing. Classmates patting him on the back, shouting his name like he was some kind of hero.

But the moment that stuck with him most was when Dr. Keene, his physics mentor, pulled him aside, her voice low.

"Travis," she whispered, gripping his arm. "Be careful. If what you've built truly works as you claim... people will kill to own it."

Her words followed him through the evening like a shadow. So much so that he was unable to fully enjoy his victory.

By the time the science fair award ceremony ended, his voice was hoarse from countlessly explaining the tech over and over with each new inquisitive person as they walked up and his hands ached from the tight gripped overenthusiastic shakings throughout the day. He packed the glasses carefully into their padded case, clutching them like a newborn child. The plaque gleamed on top of his backpack. Too tired and nervous to attend the after party, he headed out the banquet hall and towards his dorm.

The campus quad was quiet now, just music and laughter from the atrium he had just left becoming increasingly distant, the air cool and heavy with the promise of February rain. He crossed beneath the lampposts, every step echoing the thought: I did it. I actually did it.

At the dormitory steps, Travis paused. He wanted—no, needed—to tell someone. He fished out his phone. His parents first. His little sister, too. They'd laugh, they'd cheer, they'd be so proud.

He bolted up the stairs, two at a time, into the glow of the hallway light.

Back in his room, he set the case gently on his desk, powered up his laptop, and pulled up his parent's home number on his cell phone. He smiled and thought to himself 'They must have one of the last landlines in the country' as he hit the call button.

The ring tone pulsed in his ear, steady, expectant.

## Chapter 2: The Vanishing Call

The call connected with a click.

"Hello?" his mother's voice, warm and familiar, spilled through the line.

"Mom! You're not gonna believe it—I won first place! Top prize, the whole deal. They—"

The line crackled.

"Travis, that's wonderful, I—"

Static buzzed in his ear, shrill and hollow.

Then Silence.

He checked the screen: CALL FAILED.

Frowning, he tried again. One ring. Two. Dead silence. CALL FAILED. He cursed softly, tossing the phone onto the desk. He reached for his laptop to try a video call to his sister. Bars of signal winked in and out.. Campus Wi-Fi, probably overloaded from half the student body uploading selfies.

The lights flickered. Once. Twice. Then everything went black.

A knock at his door came sharp and urgently.

“Hello?” Travis called. “Power’s out. You too?”

No answer. Just a second knock, heavier this time.

Cautiously, Travis cracked the door. A man in a black suit stood there, face shadowed by the darkness his silhouette outlined by the faint light of the moon creeping in from a small window at the end of the hall. Another figure loomed just behind him.

“Travis Eugene Calder?” the man asked.

“Uh... yeah?” Travis responded out of reflex.

“Can we come in?” asked the second man

A strange feeling washed over Travis as the words of Dr. Keene suddenly came flooding back to his memory.

“Look, I don’t know. I’m tired, it’s getting late, the power’s out, and I don’t know you.”

The first man’s hand shot forward forcing the door open and Travis stumbling backwards. The second man was on him instantly. Something pressed against Travis’s mouth—chemical, sweet and choking. Then a prick to the neck. The world folded in on itself.

Brief moments of half lucidity as Travis, restrained in the back seat of an unfamiliar SUV, tried to force himself conscious. The sounds of the night would shake him awake but each time he would stir just enough to realize something was wrong. Unable to fight the chemical induced slumber that gripped him.

Distant at first, then close, muffled, frantic. He drifted in and out, head pounding, body heavy. Somewhere above him, voices barked in clipped, urgent tones.

"...contain it... no survivors..."

"...make it look like an accident..."

"...Keene's not accounted for—"

Travis opened his eyes in time to see more men in suits surrounding the building.

An explosion.

Then fire.

Windows burst outward in a bloom of glass. Screams torn to shreds by a concussive wave. The ceiling folding in like paper. Heat. Smoke. Red light flashing. Sirens wailing in the distance already too late. A blue glowing light, suited men disappearing into the blue glowing light. Then back under he went.

All Travis could do was hazily watch in brief separate moments from behind the back window of the vehicle he was in. Unsure how much he was seeing was real, how much was imagination, and how much was drug induced from whatever they had given him. Everything was so hazy and out of sequence.

Even half-conscious, Travis knew the sound: the roar of an explosion, the deep, gut-wrenching shudder that vibrated through the floor. His ears rang. The voices cut off, swallowed by the chaos and screams of those still inside. His eyes got heavy again. Silence pierced the fire. As Travis went under, the crackle and roar of the flames was all he could still hear.

Through the fog in his mind, images flickered: All his classmates and professors he had left at the party in celebration clinking glasses, the men in suits that surrounded the building.

And then—obliteration.

As far as Travis knew, everyone—gone.

Not everyone though.

Somehow, impossibly, a handful had walked away.

Dr. Keene had lingered outside, too suspiciously restless to join the revelry. When the suited men began showing up, she had ducked under a parked car, there she witnessed the explosion, flames painting her glasses red as she watched the men in suits guard the exits.

Miles Harker, Travis's best friend since Freshman Orientation, had left early, slipping away with a backpack full of leftover snacks. He'd been blocks away trying to score some weed, when the boom from the explosion rolled across the city.

Two reporters from the student paper—Anna Ruiz and James Maddox—had gone out back to smoke. Fifty feet away from the building as were the rules. They had hidden in a nearby bush when they noticed the suspicious men in suits surrounding the building. Moments later the explosion came. James had almost run toward the building when it happened. Anna grabbed his arm as he made his move and just shook her head as he looked back at her. James suddenly realized what she already had...it was too late to do anything. So, they hid and watched.

The rest?

Charred, broken, buried beneath rubble.

Travis's mind floated in the dark. The images weren't his own memories. They came to him in jagged pieces, overheard from his captors' radios, glimpses in fever-dream flashes. But with every brief moment of consciousness the truth carved itself deeper into his skull: they were erasing witnesses.

Him included.

Cold water shocked him awake.

He sputtered, coughing, gasping, chained to a steel chair. Fluorescent lights buzzed overhead, weak and yellow. The walls around him were concrete, stained with watermarks.

An interrogation room. But not the kind police used. This was older. Dirtier. The kind of place where answers were extracted, not requested.

His wrists burned where the cuffs bit into them. His mouth tasted of metal.

A door groaned open. Footsteps.

Travis forced his head up, blinking against the light. Shadows moved. The shape of a man stood just beyond the glow.

Somewhere deep inside, fear curled like a fist.

Elsewhere, the survivors, feeling lucky to be alive and totally unprepared for impending danger, scattered like leaves in a storm:

Dr. Keene, slipped into the night with her briefcase clutched tight, already planning her next move. Which was to get as far away as possible.

Miles, holed up in his dorm room after getting his smoke, phone buzzing with unanswered calls, getting baked while watching news of the "tragic gas explosion" that killed his classmates and his best friend as far as he knew.

Anna Ruiz and James Maddox, the reporters, shaken and trembling, scribbling frantic notes about what they'd seen. Men in suits on the scene moments before the explosion. How they lingered, watched, patrolled but made no efforts to save anyone. And then disappeared moments before any law enforcement or rescue personnel were present.

Each of them was alive—for now.

Each of them had seen too much.

And somewhere, in the bowels of that interrogation room, Travis Calder drew his first steady breath since winning the science fair prize... and realized he might not draw many more.

## Chapter 3: Gaslight

The light in the interrogation room never dimmed. It hummed overhead, a steady, buzzing eye that burned into the top of Travis's skull.

The man in the shadows finally stepped forward. He wore a slate-gray suit, crisp and featureless, like something ordered out of a catalog. His face was forgettable, almost too plain, as though designed to leave no impression. Huge dark lensed sunglasses covered his eyes.

"Travis Calder," the man said. His voice was even, measured. "Twenty years old. Physics undergraduate. Son of Harold and Janice Calder. Notable for..." He glanced down at a folder in his hand. "winning multiple literary and science awards all through school, being offered the highest amount of scholarships than any other graduate in the history of Northwood, making Eagle Scout, playing the part of a tree in your 2nd grade school play at Herndon Magnet, and now...an invention presented today at the LSU Science & Engineering fair."

Travis swallowed. "Who are you?"

The man's lips curved, but it wasn't a smile. "We're the people who keep order. Just consider us to be one of those secret government agencies you see in movies and television, though our exact name and affiliation should not matter to you. What matters is what you built and what we want from you."

He slid a photograph across the table. A blurred image of the Quantum Vision Glasses, snapped from the science fair.

"You've made something dangerous. Something... unstable."

"They're not dangerous," Travis said hoarsely. "They just let you look—"

"Exactly." The man interrupted as he leaned close. "And what happens when the wrong people look in the wrong places? Wars have started over less."

Outside this windowless room, the world spun on.

On Channel 9 News, anchors with solemn expressions reported live from the smoldering remains of the campus ballroom.

"...officials are calling it a tragic accident," the woman said, her makeup immaculate despite the ruin behind her. "Preliminary reports suggest a combination of faulty gas lines in the science lab and outdated wiring in the ballroom ceiling. The result was catastrophic. Over fifty students, faculty, and patrons have perished in the blast."

Her co-anchor nodded gravely. "University leaders are calling for updated safety inspections across all campus facilities."

The broadcast cut to shaky cellphone footage—flames devouring the atrium roof, firefighters dragging out charred beams. No mention of inventions. No mention of survivors. No mention of Travis Calder. No men in suits anywhere to be seen.

Just a gas leak. Just faulty wiring.

A neat explanation. A closed loop.

In a kitchen miles away, Janice Calder clutched her phone to her chest.

She'd been trying to call her son back for hours, tears filled her eyes and ran down her cheeks. The line rang and rang before dropping into voicemail. "Travis, it's Mom again. Please, just... call me back. I saw the news. I need to know you're safe."

Her husband sat silent at the table, staring at the TV with the sound off.

In the back of a beat-up sedan, James Maddox tapped furiously at his laptop. His notes were scattered, adrenaline scrawled across the screen: heard shouting—saw men in black suits—explosion wasn't accident.

Anna Ruiz, in the driver's seat, shot him a nervous glance. "James, you have to be careful. If what we saw was real—"

"It was real," James said, jaw tightened. "Gas leak, my ass. I'm not letting them bury this. Someone has to tell the truth."

He barely noticed the headlights growing larger in the rearview mirror.

The truck came out of nowhere, barreling down the dark road. A screech of tires, a sickening crunch of metal. Anna screamed as the sedan spun, glass shattering, steel folding like paper.

When the world stopped spinning, James was gone. Anna was broken, bloody. She dragged herself out of the wreckage, hoping to find help. A shadowed figure approached her. "H-help me" Anna whispered, her voice raspy. A boot was on her neck. Pressure. Anna's eyes widened, she grabbed the man's leg with her left hand. Her right hand was mangled, unable to grasp so it just pawed at the man's shoe uselessly. More pressure. Completely unable to breathe. A crunch. Anna's body went limp, her eyes rolled backward. The man walked away.

Later, the headline would read:

LSU STUDENT REPORTERS KILLED IN CAR ACCIDENT.

Cause: "Driver fatigue, loss of control."

Another neat explanation.

Back in the interrogation room, the man in the gray suit slid a small recorder across the table.

"Tell us exactly how the glasses work," he said softly. "Every equation. Every process. Leave nothing out."

Travis stared at him, confused and scared, heart hammering.

## Chapter 4: The Noose Tightens

The man in the gray suit leaned back in his chair, fingers tapping the folder like a metronome. He removed his dark sunglasses and set them on the table next to the folder. His eyes, pale and unreadable, fixed on Travis with the focus of a predator.

Travis hadn't responded to the initial questions. Maybe out of shock or fear. Maybe out of caution. Whatever the reason, enough time went by since he was asked that the man in the suit took notice of his apprehension and shifted his tone into a slightly more pleasant friendly manner.

"Let's keep this simple," he said. "Who did you tell about your invention?"

Travis's throat felt like sandpaper. "No one. Just... my mentor. Dr. Keene. She knew I was working on something."

The man scribbled a note. "And your family? Did they know?"

"Only that I was building something for the competition. Not... not the details."

Another note. Another tap of the pen. "And your friends? Your roommate? Girlfriends?"

Travis shook his head. "No. Just Keene. And maybe Miles—he saw me tinkering on them once, but he didn't understand it."

The man leaned forward, voice dropping into a near-whisper. "Think carefully, Mr. Calder. Anyone who knew, even in passing, is a liability. A risk. Loose ends are not tolerated."

A chill ran down Travis's spine. He forced himself to look away from those pale eyes. "That's all," he murmured.

The man scribbled more info down and shuffled some papers around before speaking again.

"Now, back to the science of the goggles. How do they work? What are the formulas and equations you used?"

Travis never planned to tell anyone that for fear of having his invention stolen. But now his mind was starting to adjust to the situation, the adrenaline rush was wearing off, and his ability to reason was slowly returning. He needed time to think before answering anymore questions.

"I'm not saying anything else until I see a lawyer and someone tells me what this is all about."

The man closed the folder with a snap. A patronizing smile came across his face. "Have it your way Mr. Calder, we'll verify the information that you have given us and then revisit the questions you seem hesitant to answer right now. As far as lawyers go, the situation we find ourselves in does not involve lawyers. Ever." He rose smoothly, adjusting his cuff. "In the meantime... perhaps I'll send for someone that the situation does call for. Someone who has ways of extracting truth. People find cooperation comes naturally when pain does the asking."

He let the words hang in the stale air before putting on his sunglasses and turning toward the door. The lock clanged shut behind him.

Silence pressed in on the room. Travis's heart pounded against the cuffs biting into his wrists. He stared at the steel table, breath ragged.

If I tell them everything... what then?

He pictured himself walking free, back across the quad, laughing about how it was all a misunderstanding. But even as the thought formed, it curdled. The dream like memories of the explosion on campus began to re-surface. Then combing over the conversation that had just taken place. It hit him. The man's voice lingered like poison: Loose ends are not tolerated. Anyone that *knew*...Shouldn't he have said anyone that *knows*?

He realized then, with cold certainty, that even if he poured out every secret, every formula, every design—their plans wouldn't include letting him go.

The glasses weren't just his invention anymore. They were leverage.

A sob built in his chest, but he swallowed it, clenching his jaw. Think, Travis. Think.

But his thoughts looped back to the same grim conclusion:

They would never let him leave. They couldn't.

A few blocks away from campus, Dr. Margaret Keene adjusted her scarf as she left the small cafe where she'd been hiding since the explosion. The streets were crowded, police still blocking off half the campus, students gathered, lighting candles in vigil. She kept her head down, briefcase clutched to her chest.

Her instincts screamed at her to keep moving. She'd seen men in dark coats circling the periphery of the blast site, talking into earpieces, watching faces too carefully. But that was immediately after. She hadn't spotted one in over an hour. Not since the roof of the atrium had collapsed. They all seemed to vanish as the first flashes of police, EMT, and firefighters appeared over the horizon in the distance.

She turned into an alley to cut toward her car—only to freeze.

A man stood waiting. Same slate-gray suit. Same forgettable features.

"Dr. Keene," he said, as though greeting an old friend.

Her stomach dropped. Without a word, she turned and bolted.

The man lunged, fingers grazing her coat sleeve. She twisted free, heels pounding the pavement. Her bag thudded against her ribs, breath tearing at her lungs. Behind her, the man barked something into a radio.

She ran into the street, weaving through traffic. A horn blared, brakes screeched. She dove across the hood of a car, stumbled, then sprinted the last block toward her battered sedan.

Her hands shook as she jammed the keys into the ignition. The engine coughed, sputtered, then roared to life.

In the rearview mirror, two suited men emerged from the alley, faces expressionless. One raised a phone to his ear.

Dr. Keene peeled out into the night, tires squealing.

Across the state, in Shreveport, a knock echoed at a quiet suburban door.

Janice Calder set down her tea, frowning at the hour. Through the frosted glass, two silhouettes waited on her porch.

She opened the door a crack.

“Mrs. Calder?” The taller one smiled warmly, though his eyes didn’t. “We’re with the university safety board. We just need a few moments of your time to discuss your son.”

Her heart skipped. “Travis? Is he all right?”

The shorter man’s smile widened. “He’s fine. Why don’t we come in and explain everything?”

Janice, caught between fear and hope, opened the door wider.

The men stepped inside.

# Chapter 5: No Way Out

The door groaned open, and the man in the gray suit returned. His expression was unchanged, as though time hadn't moved since he'd left. He set the folder back on the table with deliberate care.

"Ready to talk, Mr. Calder?"

Travis sat slumped in the chair, wrists raw from the cuffs. His mouth was dry, lips cracking already. But his eyes burned with something sharper now—not fear, but certainty.

"You're wasting your time," he rasped.

The man tilted his head. "Am I?"

"Yes," Travis said, louder this time. "Because I figured it out. No matter what I tell you—every formula, every note—you'll never let me walk out of here. You've been cleaning up witnesses since the science competition. I know it. You'll kill me the second I stop being useful."

The man's pale eyes didn't flicker. He simply adjusted his cufflinks. "You're not as naïve as I expected."

“Then admit it,” Travis demanded. “Admit you’re going to kill me.”

For the first time, the man allowed himself a full faced ghost of a smile. “Mr. Calder, it’s true. You’ll die when you stop being valuable. When that happens though depends entirely on you. In the meantime, you will learn that there are things far worse than death. Things that can be done to the human body and spirit that will make death seem like an optimistic delight.”

He snapped his fingers. The door opened, and another figure entered—a broader man in rolled-up sleeves, carrying a black case. He set it on the table with a heavy thud.

Travis’s stomach turned.

The case opened with a click. Inside lay instruments—not surgical, not medical, but crude. Pliers. Clamps. Needles. Wires.

The man in the suit leaned close. “Last chance Mr. Calder. Tell me how the goggles work. Or my ambitious colleague here will help you remember.”

The one that had come in with the case pulled on gloves. He was smiling maniacally with a fire in his eyes like he had just opened his favorite present on Christmas morning. The psychotic look alone was terrifying.

Travis swallowed hard, fighting the rising bile. “You’re monsters.”

“No,” the man said softly. “We’re patriots. Protectors even, some might say”

The first needle pierced flesh.

Travis screamed.

The two suited men stepped out of the Calder home, their coats buttoned. One of them pressed a phone to his ear. His voice crisp in the cool night air.

“Mission complete. Target residence was negative. No evidence of invention, or schematics. No subjects of interest.”

A pause, then: “Parents neutralized. Staged as robbery gone bad.”

Behind them, through the open front door, the faint flicker of overturned lamps cast jagged shadows across the living room. Blood pooled in the carpet. A family photo lay shattered on the floor, smiling faces trapped beneath broken glass.

One of the men closed the door gently behind them. As they walked down the driveway, a child screamed from inside the house. "Ready team two, prepare to intercept 911 call from residence."

The night was quiet at Miles Harker's apartment. He sat cross-legged on the couch, exhausted from emotion, the TV muted, the glow painting his tired face. His laptop was open; half a dozen tabs filled the screen with news articles about the "tragic campus gas explosion."

He couldn't make sense of it. None of it fit.

The clock ticked past midnight.

Then—three sharp knocks rattled the door.

Miles froze.

Another knock. Louder.

His throat went dry. Slowly, he stood, heart hammering in his chest, and stared at the door handle.

## Chapter 6: Breaking Point

Travis hung limp in the chair, head bowed. Blood streaked down his face in rivulets, drying in dark patterns across his shirt. His wrists were swollen from the cuffs, his breathing ragged and shallow. Every inch of him burned, stitched with raw lines of pain from the hours of needles, clamps, and wires. His voice had broken long ago—now it came out in cracked whispers and sobs.  Still, he had told them nothing. He figured if death was the worst they could do, he would keep his lips shut and wait for it patiently.

The door opened with a hiss.

The man in the gray suit stepped inside, his shoes clicking against the concrete. He closed the door gently, almost tenderly, before speaking.

"That's enough," he said. His voice was calm, like a father stopping a scolding gone too far. "Your tolerance for pain is very impressive Mr. Calder. So, we're going to try something else now."

He gestured. The broad man in sleeves returned, dragging someone with him.

Travis's blurry eyes widened.

"M-Miles?"

Miles Harker stumbled as he was being pushed into the room, bound at the wrists, gag shoved between his teeth. His eyes were wide, frantic, darting between Travis and the men holding him. His muffled cries came out desperate and wet against the cloth.

Travis struggled against the cuffs. "No! No, he doesn't know anything! He didn't do anything!"

The man in the suit crouched beside him, studying Travis with detached interest. "Pain can be abstract, Mr. Calder. Numbers, equations, even broken bones can all be confusing. But sometimes one's own clarity comes faster when the consequences are more...personal."

Travis spat blood in his direction. "Go to hell."

The man stood, unfazed, and in one smooth motion drew a pistol from his jacket. The barrel gleamed in the light as he pressed it against Miles's temple.

Miles thrashed, whimpering into the gag, eyes begging Travis to do something. Anything.

"Stop!" Travis screamed, straining against the cuffs until his skin tore. "Don't you dare—don't you fucking dare!"

The man's pale eyes held his. "Then tell me what I need to know."

"Please! He doesn't—he's my best friend, he doesn't deserve this!"

A pause.

"Not what I asked you Mr. Calder."

Then a gunshot.

The crack split the room. Blood splattered across the concrete. Miles went still, crumpling to the ground like a marionette with its strings cut.

Travis howled, the sound torn from the deepest pit of his chest. He cursed as the broad man drug Miles's lifeless body out of the room by his feet. Until his throat shredded, until the words blurred into animal noise.

The man in the suit calmly wiped the barrel of his gun with a handkerchief, then produced a small tablet from his pocket. He tapped the screen, then turned it toward Travis.

A video feed filled the display: a girl no older than twelve, sitting in the back seat of a car, clutching a stuffed animal to her chest. Her face was pale, her eyes red from crying.

Travis froze.

"L-Lydia..."

The man's voice was smooth, matter-of-fact. "Your sister. Right now, she believes she's being taken to the police station. Those men in the front seat." He nodded toward the screen. "They work for me. They told her she's being taken to wait while they locate her next of kin. That's you, isn't it? I wonder what will become of Lydia when they can't find you. Best case scenario, a distant Aunt. Can you think of any loving long lost relatives you may have, Mr. Calder? No? Well then, the most likely scenario, she goes to a foster home and into the system. Her odds of leading a great life aren't overwhelmingly positive...But she still has a shot because she's still in the game. Now, let me tell you the worst-case scenario Mr. Calder, we bring her here and nobody ever sees her again. Nobody except for you as you're strapped to that chair watching us do vile despicable things to her. Day after day. Over and again. Until we all grow bored with her. Comforting thoughts, aren't they? So, Mr. Calder, where are we taking young Lydia? What fate will you seal for her?"

Travis's stomach lurched. The realization hit him like a dump truck. "You son of a bitch. You fucking monster. You're saying you've already killed my parents? You—"

The man raised a hand, silencing him. "What's done is done. I suggest you shift your attention to Lydia. She's had a difficult day already. Would be a shame to compound it. If you cooperate, Mr. Calder, my men will deliver her safely into police custody. If not..."

He motioned to the empty chair that sat across from Travis. "You get a front row seat. Years of abuse. Until. One bullet. Right through that tiny head. We don't enjoy the torturing or disposing of children, but we won't hesitate to do so either. We will do anything to protect our interest."

Travis's vision blurred, tears spilling hot and furious down his blood-caked cheeks. He pulled at the cuffs until his flesh split anew, screamed every curse word he knew at the man—words like broken glass hurled against stone.

The man only waited, watching him unravel.

Finally, Travis sagged, defeated. His chest heaved with each breath, his spirit clawed hollow.

“Fine. What do you want me to do?” he whispered.

The man smiled faintly, slipping the tablet back into his coat. “That’s much better Mr. Calder. Now, back to the technology of these goggles...”

While Travis’s world collapsed in that concrete room, Dr. Margaret Keene was already vanishing.

Her sedan hugged the backroads, taillights swallowed by the dark Louisiana pines. The city was shrinking in her rearview mirror, the skyline just a memory.

She flung her phone into a drainage ditch at mile marker 42, switched out her license plate with a vehicle that looked like hers at a Lake

Charles Wal-Mart, maxed out the cash advance of her credit cards at a gas station ATM in Beaumont Texas, then doubled back and drove right back through Baton Rouge in the opposite direction. Hoping she had gone far enough one way to lead anyone searching for her in the wrong direction.

As she made her way through town, she couldn't help but drive past the burnt remains of the LSU science building one more time. A reminder of all the people gone, and the fact that she needed to run and hide.

By dawn, she would be gone—no forwarding address, no paper trail. Just another ghost on the backroads of America.

Her only chance of survival was to disappear before they found her.

And she knew they would be looking.

# Chapter 7: The New World

**April 21st 2042**

Fifteen years have passed since the invention of the Quantum Vision Goggles.

Almost no one had ever heard the name Travis Calder. His photograph had vanished from public record. His family, too. All that remained was the invention—polished, branded, and owned exclusively by the government.

The Quantum Vision System™ was celebrated as humanity's greatest leap forward. Crime rates had plummeted. Alibis were confirmed with absolute certainty. Cold cases thawed and closed by the thousands. Trials ended in days, not months. Caged innocents were freed. Murderers no longer hid behind lies. The quantum vision goggles were the best tools law enforcement had ever received. And that was the primary function of the goggles.

Once a year however, the goggles were released under strict supervision to handpicked universities, where bright young History majors could "see history" as part of their academic tours. A gift to the next generation. A gesture meant to present government transparency. And a reminder that truth was easily determined.

The world seemed brighter. Safer. Cleaner. Almost utopian.

Alex Monroe, a highly intelligent kid but lack luster student with scruffy hair, adjusted the strap of his backpack as he shuffled onto the bus with the rest of his history class. The bus pulled out onto the road and away from the University of Alabama. Many hours, conversations, and naps later the salty breeze of Massachusetts Bay slapped his face, tangling his hair. Ahead, waves lapped gently against the worn granite slab of Plymouth Rock.

He'd seen it in textbooks, glossy photographs that made it look majestic. In person, it was smaller than he expected. Just a stone, roped off and fenced in, sitting like an oversized gravestone at the edge of the sea.

Still, the sight made his stomach flutter. Today wasn't about the rock. It was about what they would see through the goggles.

"Line up, everyone!" Professor Daniels barked, his voice half drowned by the gulls overhead. He was a tall man with a booming laugh, the kind of teacher who lived for days like this.

Alex fell into line with his classmates, more interested in watching government handlers unload sleek black cases from an armored van parked nearby. The cases were marked with the silver emblem of the Department of Temporal Oversight—DTO for short. Their motto was stenciled beneath in tidy block letters:

TRUTH THROUGH VISION.

Two agents in dark suits supervised as the cases were clicked open, revealing rows of Quantum Vision Goggles. These weren't the clunky prototypes Travis Calder had once built. These were elegant—streamlined silver frames with iridescent lenses, thin as dragonfly wings.

One by one, students were fitted with their sets.

When Alex's turn came, he held his breath as the agent placed the goggles gently over his eyes. A faint hum vibrated against his temples. The air shimmered. For a second, he saw his own reflection in the lenses of the agent standing over him—then the world melted.

The gulls vanished. The tide rolled backward. The space around him shimmered a light blue as the light seemed to bend around nothing. The horizon changed.

Suddenly, he stood in the year 1620. The beach was crowded with weary, pale-faced settlers in rough woolen clothes. They dragged supplies across the sand, their breath white in the chill air. Children cried. Men shouted orders in accents strange and old-fashioned.

And there—anchored in the harbor—was the Mayflower, sails furled, towering like a ghostly cathedral on the water.

Alex gasped. "It's real..."

Beside him, his classmates murmured in awe, each seeing the same scene play out from the same vantage point. Some laughed nervously, others wiped tears from their eyes.

Professor Daniels raised his arms like a conductor. "Students! We are witnessing the arrival of the Pilgrims at Plymouth Rock! Remember, what we are seeing is not a reenactment, it's not a recording—it is history itself! Isn't this magnificent!?"

The settlers moved among them, oblivious to the invisible audience. A man bent to lift a child onto his shoulders, right through where Alex stood.

The professor's voice softened. "Breathe it in ladies and gentlemen. This is the gift of the Quantum Vision. The truth of our past, our own origin story, alive before our very eyes."

The goggles clicked off with a soft pulse.

The settlers, the ship, the beach—they all dissolved, leaving Alex blinking at the present-day granite stone, the waves lapping, the gulls wheeling overhead again. His classmates erupted into excited chatter, giddy and breathless.

"Did you see the little girl crying?"

"Her dress looked so itchy!"

"The Mayflower—it was so much smaller than I thought!"

Professor Daniels clapped his hands. "And that, my students, is only the beginning. Tomorrow, we'll stand on the fields of Gettysburg. Next week, the steps of the Lincoln

Memorial. We are about to walk through the living record of our nation."

Alex tugged the goggles off and stared at them in his hands. Sleek, shining, flawless.

And yet... something about the way the agents hovered, the way their eyes scanned the crowd—not the stone, not the sea, but the students—sent a shiver down his spine.

## Chapter 8: Windows Into the Past

The tour bus smelled faintly of diesel fuel and snack wrappers, the air thick with chatter as Professor Daniels paced the aisle with the restless energy of a man in love with his own syllabus.

"Remember, class, every site we visit isn't just history—it's truth. What the Quantum Vision shows us is immune to bias, interpretation, or rumor. It is the raw, unfiltered record of humanity itself!"

"Yeah, unless someone in our class sneezes or farts right as Lincoln gives the Gettysburg Address," muttered Alex's friend Noah from the row behind him. A ripple of laughter ran down the seats.

Daniels ignored the jab, beaming as the bus slowed to a stop. "And here we are—the hallowed fields of Gettysburg."

The students filed out, DTO agents forming their usual perimeter. At this stop, a black case containing a fresh set of goggles would be assigned and distributed to each student. Having successfully completed their tutorials at the first stop, they would be responsible for operating and keeping up with their own pair from here on out. Still under the overly watchful eyes of the DTO, of course. Soon, the hum of activation washed over them.

The green hills shimmered, and suddenly the land boiled with soldiers in blue and gray. Cannon smoke curled across the ridges. Men shouted, fired, fell. Horses screamed. They could almost smell the stench of gunpowder and sweat which seemed to cling to the air itself.

Alex winced as a soldier that wasn't really there, collapsed at his feet, blood soaking the grass where he stood. He looked up and saw a line of Union troops charging straight through where some of his classmates lingered, their spectral faces taut with terror.

"Holy crap," whispered Maya, the girl beside him. "This is... it's like being inside a nightmare."

"It's awesome," Noah corrected, wide-eyed. "Like Call of Duty but real."

Professor Daniels's voice quavered with reverence. "Never forget, students—these aren't actors. These are the dead, still fighting their war.

Ready and willing to lay down their life to protect the future and freedoms we enjoy today."

Daniels paused for effect. Once he felt his words had adequately sunken in he continued. "Now return your goggles to their protective case. These will be your goggles for the remainder of the trip. We've all seen the tutorials and signed the agreement. So then you know, they are only to come out of the case when they are to be used, and they are only to be used when instructed by myself or one of the other faculty and/or DTO officers is present. Understood?"

When the goggles powered down, some of the students were pale, others buzzing with adrenaline. Alex found his hands trembling. He wasn't sure if it was awe or horror.

Their next stop was Washington, D.C. The steps of the Lincoln Memorial.

Again, the goggles shimmered, and suddenly Martin Luther King Jr. stood before a vast sea of humanity, voice rolling like thunder: "I have a dream..."

The crowd roared, fists pumping, flags waving. Alex felt his chest tighten. He had read the speech a dozen times in textbooks, heard recordings in class, but standing in the sea of faces, hearing the power shake the air—it was like the words lived in his blood.

Katie reached up and brushed a tear away quickly, embarrassed over the fact humanity had once been so bad that Dr. King's speech even need existed. Trying to accept the fact that whole groups of people had been treated so poorly by her ancestors. Remembering that this was only one of many instances.

Noah only whispered, "Damn."

When the vision ended, the DTO agents were quick to usher them back toward the bus, eyes scanning the crowd of tourists who weren't part of the program. Ensuring that the goggles were being safely and securely placed back in their cases.

Alex, having only pushed his goggles up over his forehead, noticed one agent lingering near him. A tall man with a square jaw, mirrored sunglasses, and an earpiece. As Alex tried to step past, the man's hand shot out, stopping him with a firm press to the chest.

"Young man," the agent said flatly. "Keep your goggles secure at all times. They are not toys. Understood?"

Alex stammered, as he removed the goggles and put them in his case, "Y-yes, sir."

The agent leaned closer, his breath warm, his words clipped. "What you see is a privilege, not a right. Remember that."

Then he let him go.

Alex hurried back onto the bus, cheeks burning. His friends didn't notice, but the agent's warning echoed in his brain all the way down the highway.

Days passed in a blur of sites: Independence Hall, the Trail of Tears, the Wright Brothers' flight at Kitty Hawk. The students joked, argued, shared earbuds, and swapped snacks, but each new window into history left its own mark—some awe, some unease.

And always, the agents stood nearby, silent and watchful.

When the bus finally crossed into Texas, the atmosphere shifted.

DTO vehicles flanked them now—black SUVs with tinted windows. At the motel, uniformed guards patrolled the lot, handlers shadowed every table, their eyes constantly flicking to the cases of goggles as though they were nuclear launch codes.

Even Professor Daniels seemed subdued, his usual booming laugh replaced with careful explanations of protocol.

"Tomorrow," he said quietly as the bus cruised along interstate 20 into Dallas, "we will be observing the assassination of President John F. Kennedy. For reasons that should be obvious, security protocols will be tighter than usual. You will always remain in groups of at least two, wherever you go. You will not wander far from the group during the day. You will have a 12 o'clock curfew tonight. And you will treat what you see tomorrow with the utmost respect."

Alex glanced out the window. The DTO presence was heavier than ever—agents on rooftops, agents at every intersection, their black coats stark against the Texas sun.

Something about it felt wrong.

As the bus pulled up to Dealey Plaza, Alex's stomach knotted. The laughter and chatter that had filled the ride was gone now, replaced with a nervous hush.

He clutched his goggle case in both hands, a chill running down his spine.

## Chapter 9: Off the Leash

The bus hissed as it pulled into the hotel parking lot, the DTO convoy fanning out like a military escort. Black SUVs prowled the curb. Armed men in dark jackets rounded the building, their eyes never still.

Professor Daniels rose as the students gathered their bags. His voice was lower than usual, weighty with importance.

"Tomorrow," he said, "you will witness one of the most painful, pivotal moments in American history—the assassination of President John F. Kennedy. Because of the sensitivity of this event and the usual heavy traffic flow of the site area, the DTO has implemented heightened security. Your goggles will remain locked in their cases tonight, secured in your rooms. Guards will be posted on every floor. I repeat: no goggles outside of designated viewing hours. And remember the curfew."

He paused, sweeping the bus with his gaze. "You've all been exemplary students on this tour. Don't spoil it now by testing limits. We want to observe history, not become a headline."

A nervous chuckle rippled through the bus.

The hotel itself was modern but cold, its wide glass lobby dominated by a DTO checkpoint. Students filed through metal detectors, guards tagging each case of goggles with biometric locks. This was not new procedure.

Alex trailed behind his group, watching as the agents checked every latch, every seam of the storage cases. They weren't just protective—they were paranoid. This level of paranoia was new.

Up in the room, Noah flopped onto his bed, arms spread wide. "Finally, a night off. Daniels seemed serious, though. We should probably just grab food and chill."

But Alex's mind was already elsewhere. He kept replaying the words: locked in their cases... secured in your rooms. He knew the locks, knew the safeguards. But he also liked to break the rules for the sake of a good time. He felt he knew the goggles inside and out.

And he'd noticed something the agents hadn't about the biometric locks on the cases.

An hour later, Alex and a small group of classmates went out into the Dallas night. Him, Noah, Brian, Maya, and Katie. They all did stuff together often. Well, except for Katie, who had recently been befriended by Maya. She was new to the group and still a little withdrawn from the other members of the group.

As they exited the hotel lobby Alex felt a brief moment of nausea accompanied by an intense feeling of de ja vu and considered turning back. But the feeling quickly passed, and he continued onward with the rest of his group.

The city was alive with neon, the air warm and humming with traffic. DTO men stood at the hotel doors, nodding curtly as they left.

As they passed Dealey Plaza, Alex slowed. Bright floodlights washed the grassy knoll, DTO technicians moving briskly with coils of cable and tall antennae. Strange tripod rigs stood like spindly skeletons; their lenses aimed at the plaza.

"What's all this?" Alex whispered to his group.

Before anyone could answer, a guard snapped, "Keep moving!" His voice was sharp, his hand already clutching his sidearm.

Alex swallowed and quickened his pace. But his eyes lingered on the strange rigs being erected. Something about them unsettled him, though he couldn't say why.

The group ended up at a hole in the wall bar, IDs waved through without question—college kids with money were always welcome. Music throbbed, neon buzzed, glasses clinked.

Alex nursed a beer, waiting for the moment.

Finally, when the laughter was high and the group loose, he leaned forward and dropped the bomb. "What if I told you I brought the goggles?"

The table went quiet. Maya's eyebrows shot up. "No. You didn't."

Alex grinned, reaching into his jacket and producing the sleek, black headset. "Told you the biometric locks were a joke."

Noah nearly spit out his beer. "Dude, you're insane. Daniels would kill you."

"Only if he finds out." Alex set the goggles in the center of the table like contraband. "So... what do y'all want to see? Where should we go?"

Ideas flew like sparks. All trying to remember important historical events relative to the area. The annexation of Oak Cliff, the 1908 Great Trinity River Flood, the creation of Love Field in 1917.

Katie was nervous about being part of the rule breaking but remained quiet which was typical for her. She was just happy to be part of a group for once.

The only other person that truly knew Katie was Tricia, who herself was very reclusive when it came to socializing with her peers. Tricia had no interest in being included in anything Katie was doing with her new friends and elected to stay behind telling Katie to "Be careful" as she left her room that evening.

Then Brian—the diehard Cowboys fan—leaned forward, eyes shining. "I've got it. AT&T Stadium. January 28th, 1996. Last time we won the Super Bowl. I've dreamt of seeing a Cowboy's Super Bowl win, live in person, my whole life."

Groans and laughter circled the table.

Still, curiosity won. Feeling this may break the monotony of educational viewings. They piled into a rideshare, whooping and singing as the city blurred by. Soon, they were standing in the shadow of the great stadium, its lights off, the parking lot empty.

Brian's hands trembled and his heart raced as he dialed the date with ceremonial precision, and placed the goggles on his head. "This is it," he whispered. "My kind of history."

The headset hummed, the shimmer began the light bent until he was looking at—

—nothing.

Just the cold, dark emptiness of the night. No players. No fans. No triumphant victory. Not even a stadium or parking lot.

Brian blinked, adjusted, tried again. Still nothing.

Noah doubled over, howling with laughter. "Oh my God. You picked the wrong date!"

"I did not!" Brian's face flushed red.

Maya was giggling too, while researching on her smart phone. "The Super Bowl was in Arizona that year, genius. Not Dallas. And this stadium hadn't even been built!"

The teasing rolled over him in waves. "Even with time goggles, you can't see the Cowboys win a Super Bowl!" Noah crowed, nearly falling to the ground.

With that, Alex laughed until his sides ached. For one glorious moment, the tension of DTO guards and somber history dissolved into pure, ridiculous joy.

They spent the rest of the night bar-hopping, drinking, daring each other to try songs at karaoke joints. The goggles stayed tucked away, but the secret of them buzzed between the group like electricity.

Maya even had the idea at one point of suggesting they try to use the goggles to look into the future. They had been told it was not possible, but shouldn't they at least try?

Katie squirmed at the idea. Something about it didn't feel right. But, as usual, Katie remained quiet.

Alex, intrigued by the idea decided to set the dials for five minutes ahead of them but when he fired them up, the lens just went black and flashed:

Error Code: RT-9-10-2027-1-47-PM

He tried again, three more times in fact, different future date and time.

Same exact error code each time.

Error Code: RT-9-10-2027-1-47-PM

At last, swaying and stumbling, they decided to head back.

The hotel loomed ahead, black DTO SUVs still idling, guards still watchful. The laughter faded as they approached, each student sobering to the sight.

Alex tucked the goggles back into his jacket, pulse quickening. He had gotten away with it—for now.

But something about the glow of Dealey Plaza, still lit by DTO rigs in the distance, gnawed at him.

Something was different about this historical viewing.

# Chapter 10: The Shot No One Saw

The laughter and teasing of earlier had faded, replaced with a gnawing curiosity he couldn't silence.

Tomorrow the class will see the JFK assassination. But tomorrow, everything will be controlled—timed, supervised, smoothed into the narrative the DTO had sanctioned.

Tonight, though... tonight he had the goggles. Tonight, he could look for himself.

He slipped away quietly from the group. Hid. Waited for his drunken friends to head back into the hotel, to their rooms. Making sure nobody noticed he was missing. No one did. They were too occupied with the DTO agents and trying to maintain the illusion they were sober.

Dealey Plaza was hushed, the floodlights casting long shadows across the grassy knoll. The strange tripod rigs stood silent now, their lights off but their presence menacing. Alex ducked behind a low stone wall, crouching in the dark.

Hands trembling, he pulled on the goggles and scrolled the dial. November 22, 1963. 12:30 p.m.

The world shimmered.

And then he was there.

Crowds lined the street, their voices bright with anticipation. The air was alive with cheers, children running around with excitement or being lifted onto their fathers' shoulders, women waving handkerchiefs and checking their makeup as if the President would take notice when he rode by. A motorcade glided into view, sunlight flashing on polished chrome.

The President's car.

JFK sat smiling and waving, Jackie radiant as always beside him. The air vibrated with the joy of the crowd.

Alex swallowed hard. He knew what was coming.

He turned his head toward the Texas School Book Depository, focusing on the sixth-floor window where history had recorded Lee Harvey Oswald's rifle.

The window was cracked open, curtains fluttering. A pale face appeared, cautious, eyes scanning. Alex's breath caught.

But then—

Movement.

On the grassy knoll.

At first, Alex thought it was a trick of the light. But no—the air shimmered, a more electric blue than what he had seen previously through the goggles, and more densely concentrated in a small area. It rippled like heat haze. A circle of energy bloomed against the shadows, a portal yawning open.

And a man stepped out.

Dark suit. Earpiece. No official markings, but he had the generic look of a DTO officer.

Alex's stomach dropped. At first, he thought the agent was there for him. That he had been busted.

The agent stopped, knelt smoothly, pulling a rifle from nowhere, raising it with mechanical precision.

Oswald saw him too.

From the window, the supposed assassin froze, eyes wide. His lips moved—"What the hell—?" He fumbled for his rifle, confusion on his face, anger blooming, signs of panic.

He wasn't aiming at the President. He was aiming at the man on the knoll.

But the agent was faster.

The shot rang out, deafening. Kennedy's head snapped back, blood poured from the wound, eyes glassing over. Jackie's scream tearing through the air. The crowd erupted, chaos surging like a tidal wave. Joy replaced with anarchy within seconds.

Oswald, shaking, fired—once, twice—his bullets sparking harmlessly off the stone as the agent stepped calmly back into the glowing circle. In a blink, the portal sealed shut.

And he was gone.

Oswald shrieked, pounding the windowsill, pointing where he had seen the gunman seemingly disappear into nothing, "It wasn't me! I was trying to stop him!" His voice was hoarse, wild.

Police swarmed the building. Shouts, boots on stairs as they charged upward, orders barked. In minutes Oswald was dragged down, screaming, spitting, trying to explain—"A man, he had a gun! He vanished into a blue hole! You don't understand, I was protecting him! I'm on a secret mission! I was hired to protect the President! I'm a fucking patriot!"

But no one listened. To them, he was just another assassin, another madman.

The history Alex had always been told—the one etched into textbooks—was not what he had just seen. Questions began to fill his inebriated mind.

Was it all a lie? Who was that man that came out of nowhere? How *had* he come out of nowhere? Who sent him? Was he part of the DTO? These were the questions swirling around his brain.

Alex yanked the goggles off, gasping. His chest felt tight, his hands numb. The plaza around him was empty again, silent except for the faint hum of generators on the DTO rigs.

He staggered to his feet, clutching the goggles like contraband on fire. Every nerve in his body screamed to run.

And run he did.

Through the shadows, past the guards at the corner, back into the artificial safety of the hotel. His pulse thundered as he slipped into his room and collapsed onto the bed.

Noah stirred, grunted, rolled over.

Alex lay staring into the dark, the memory of the shot echoing in his ears.

The world believed Oswald was guilty. History taught us he was guilty.

But Alex had seen otherwise. Contradictory to history itself...

Alex knew the truth.

And if the DTO had erased that truth, what else had they buried?

His stomach, queasy, as he squeezed the goggles tighter against his chest. He was no longer worried about detentions, grades, or Daniels's scolding.

Now, all he feared was being caught by the DTO. And what would happen to him if they found out what he had done...what he had seen.

## Chapter 11: Eyes on the Knoll

The hotel lobby buzzed with nervous energy. Students clustered in groups, chattering, laughing too loudly, disguising their unease of what they were preparing to see with false bravado. Professor Daniels stood by the entrance, clipboard in hand, fussing over attendance like it was any ordinary field trip.

But nothing about this morning felt ordinary.

Black SUVs still idled outside. Armed DTO agents formed a living barrier between the students and the city beyond. Their rifles hung at ease, but their eyes were restless, scanning, recording. This was something new.

Alex felt each gaze like a spotlight, wondering if the armored agents were there for him because of what he had seen or if it was to make sure everybody saw what they wanted them to. The only thing he knew for sure was they were up to something. He adjusted the strap of his backpack, trying to look casual as the line shuffled forward.

Dealey Plaza looked different in daylight. The sun cast sharp shadows across the street, and the white pergola gleamed stark against the grass. But the odd rigs Alex had seen last night were still there—tripods, coils of thick cable, tall antennae like skeletal fingers pointing skyward.

This time, though, they weren't shadowed in secrecy.

A DTO officer addressed the class in clipped tones. "For your safety and the integrity of this experience, supplemental equipment has been deployed. These measures prevent outside interference from the noise and light of the city and stabilize the historical reconstruction. You will not touch any of the equipment and you will remain within the designated perimeter at all times. Understood?"

A chorus of uneasy nods followed.

Alex's throat went dry. 'Supplemental equipment.' So that's what they were calling it.

He slipped on his goggles with trembling hands.

The shimmer came, and the world tilted.

Crowds lined the streets, cheering. The motorcade rolled slowly toward the plaza, sunshine bouncing off polished chrome. Jackie's pink suit was as radiant as he remembered from the previous night; her gloved hand raised in a wave. So far following everything Alex had seen the previous evening.

Everyone in the class was watching, their attention darting back and forth between the parade and the window of the 6th floor where Oswald would be.

Alex's stomach knotted. His gaze slid toward the grassy knoll where he had seen the real assassin emerge the night before.

Nothing.

No shimmer. No portal. Just a fence, a patch of grass, and ordinary people waving their flags.

His heart thudded harder. Had he imagined it all? An intoxicated illusion perhaps?

Then—out of the corner of his left goggled eye—he caught the smallest movement among the DTO agents stationed nearby. Two of them had noticed him staring. Their hands went to radios, murmuring low into their sleeves.

Alex swallowed hard and forced his eyes forward. Towards Kennedy and Oswald. Kennedy came rolling by. Back at the window, Oswald with panicked look and rifle poking out. He fired two rounds.

The shots rang.

JFK collapsed into Jackie's arms, the crowd's joy exploded into screams. Chaos. Running. People dropping to the ground, covering their children. Sirens wailing in the distance.

Alex kept his face neutral, jaw clenched, though every instinct screamed to look back at the knoll. To confirm. To scream the truth.

But he didn't.

He couldn't.

When the vision ended, the plaza was once again quiet. The class staggered, some pale, some shaking, others chattering nervously.

"Oh my God..." Maya whispered. "That was real. That really happened right here."

Noah rubbed his arms, trying to laugh it off. "History sucks, man. Why couldn't we just watch them shoot Harambe or something?"

The DTO agents herded the group back toward the buses. Alex drug behind, pulse hammering, still fighting the urge to glance over his shoulder.

That's when someone slipped into step beside him.

"Don't look around," the voice said softly.

Alex flinched. An older woman in a plain tourist's jacket, her hair streaked with gray, walked calmly at his side. Her face was lined but sharp, her eyes piercing beneath the brim of her cap.

It was Dr. Keene.

"I saw you watching the wrong direction. So did the DTO agents. Like you were waiting for something to happen" she said under her breath. "Which means you either saw something you weren't supposed to or know something you shouldn't. If that's true, they'll know. They always find out."

Alex's chest tightened. "What—who are you—"

"Listen," she cut him off. "You're in danger. Right now, you need to act normal. Do you understand? Normal."

He nodded stiffly, terror spiking through him.

"Good. Tonight, midnight. Cocoa Beach Pier, at your next stop in Florida. Don't tell your friends. Don't bring the goggles. Just you." Her voice was sharp, final. "If you want to live, you'll be there."

And just like that, she peeled away, vanishing into the dispersing crowd.

Moments later, Alex was back on the bus with the others. His palms were slick with sweat. His classmates were buzzing about Kennedy, about Jackie's scream, about how the reality or presence felt compared to classroom study of the history books.

But Alex barely heard them.

He only heard Dr. Keene's warning echoing in his skull.

As the bus pulled away, Professor Daniels announced their final stop with somber reverence.

"Tomorrow," he said, "we travel to Florida. To Cape Canaveral. To witness the launch of Apollo 11—the day humankind first set foot on the moon."

"Supposedly!" Noah yelled out. "I'll believe it when I see it!"

The bus erupted with chatter and laughter.

Even Professor Daniels smiled. "Finally, you will see for yourself and stop interrupting my class with your conspiracy theories!" he fired back.

Everyone laughed again. Giddy with a mix of the lighthearted banter exchanged between Professor & student that had just occurred and all the wonderfully magnificent things they had seen through the goggles on their trip.

Alex just stared out the window, fists clenched in his lap.

The grassy knoll was already fading behind them.

But the danger seemed to be looming ahead.

# Chapter 12: Echoes in the Code

**March 2027 (Exact Date Unknown)**

The room smelled of bleach and iron.

Travis sat hunched in a chair, his wrists raw where restraints had rubbed them. Around him, whiteboards crowded the walls, each scrawled with formulas, diagrams, and notes in cramped handwriting—his handwriting, though he barely remembered writing them.

Two guards and three men in lab coats hovered nearby, watching as he explained for the hundredth time the core principle of the goggles.

"...it's about resonance," Travis muttered, his voice hoarse. "Quantum fields can be indexed by time as well as space. The goggles—just align perception with the residue of what's already happened. The lattice still holds the echoes. It's like tuning a radio, but the signal is the past itself."

The scientists scribbled. Unseen men behind the glass leaned forward.

Travis lifted a hand, pointing at a formula smeared across the board. “These alloys stabilize the field. Without them, the lens burns out. With them, you can hold a vision indefinitely.”

He dropped the marker, his fingers trembling. His voice cracked. “You’ve already taken everything. What else do you want?”

**Months later...**

Travis sat at a workbench, tools scattered, circuits glowing faintly. His hair was longer, dark circles carved beneath his eyes. He soldered a delicate filament into place, the sleek black frame of a new pair of goggles gleaming beneath the harsh light.

DTO guards flanked the door.

“Faster,” one barked. “We need a working prototype by next week.”

Travis said nothing. His hands moved automatically, a craftsman enslaved to his own genius.

The goggles looked different now—refined, weaponized. These were not tools for discovery. They were instruments of control.

**That same night...**

Cold stone floor. A narrow cot. The stink of mildew and iron bars.

Travis lay in his prison cell, staring through the small barred window at the vast night sky. His lips moved silently, naming constellations, calculating latitude. Trying to figure out where in the world they had taken him.

His ribs ached when he breathed. His wrists bore scars from cuffs.

Still, in the silence, he whispered to the stars. "One day. Someone will know. Someone will see. Someone will find me."

**Days later...**

A computer lab. Code spilled across the screen in tight green rows. Travis typed with mechanical precision, the guards behind him impatient.

"Faster," one snapped again.

But Travis was already miles ahead of them.

Hidden deep in the program's bones, tucked between innocuous subroutines, he embedded fragments of truth. Warnings. Coordinates. A map disguised as error messages. Anyone unskilled that stumbled on to the anomalies would think them glitches. But if decoded properly, they whispered a destination.  A place that was particularly special to Travis.

His eyes burned. His fingers flew.

He left breadcrumbs in the machine.

Meanwhile...

A marketplace halfway around the world. Heat beamed down on the dusty street, vendors calling over their stalls. The smell of cumin and roasted meat filled the air. Local merchants shouting their deals to persuade the crowd to patronize their booth.

Dr. Keene—hair dyed, clothes plain—moved carefully between stands, eyes washing over the crowd in waves, a basket on her arm. She had learned to keep her head down. To smile just enough. To live like a shadow.

But then she saw them.

Three men in black suits, scanning faces, moving like wolves through the crowd.

Her heart clenched. Acting quickly, she ducked into a narrow shop, the air thick with incense. Shelves were stacked high with carved trinkets and old books, exotic jewelry displayed on a counter.

An older woman stepped from behind the counter, her eyes sharp and kind. “You’re being hunted,” she said, her voice low.

Keene froze. “How do you—”

“There’s no time.” The woman grabbed her wrist. “Do you want to lose them?”

“Yes,” Keene whispered. “But—”

“Then follow me.”

The woman pulled her into a back room, cluttered with crates. And there—glowing faintly against the far wall—was a circle of light. A portal, swirling with energy, humming softly like a heartbeat.

Keene staggered back. "What is this?"

The old woman's grip tightened. "I know this seems strange, Dr. Keene, but I'm here to help. You must trust me. Go through portal."

Footsteps thundered in front of the shop. The men's voices were close now, hard, demanding.

Keene hesitated, torn between terror and disbelief. Almost completely overcome with a feeling of nausea and déjà vu.

The old woman shoved her gently but firmly toward the light.

"Now."

Together, they stepped into the portal.

The energy snapped shut behind them just as the men burst into the back room, weapons drawn.

The space was empty.

## Chapter 13: The Future and the Cell

The world on the other side of the portal was blinding white for a moment, then sharp and alien.

Dr. Keene stumbled, clutching the old woman's arm. Her head spun, her stomach twisted like she'd been dropped from a great height.

"Where—" she gasped. "What—what was that?"

The old woman steadied her, her face calm, resolute. "That was survival. And this..." She gestured to the space around them. "...is safety. For now."

Keene blinked hard, trying to make sense of her surroundings. They were in a cavernous underground chamber lit with strips of pale blue light. Humming consoles lined the walls, and people in simple gray uniforms moved briskly, each with purpose.

"Who are you?" Keene demanded, her voice sharp with adrenaline. "Who are these people? Where are we?"

The old woman gave the faintest of smiles. “You can call me L. As for where—we are in an outpost, hidden from the DTO. And as for when...”

Keene’s heart hammered. “When?”

L’s eyes were steady. “The year is 2180.”

The words landed like stones in Keene’s chest. She staggered back, shaking her head. “No. That’s impossible. That’s—”

“You just walked through the impossible.”

Keene pressed her hands to her temples. “Time travel. It’s real? You—people—figured it out?”

“He figured it out over a century ago,” L corrected. “Travis. Your student. The young man who invented the goggles.”

Keene’s breath caught. “Travis? But—but the goggles only see. They don’t move. They don’t—”

L raised a hand. “He cracked the code, or will crack it, depending how you measure time. In our timeline the DTO have had complete control over the technology until rather recently. They have used it to benefit special interest groups and keep control over everyone else. All attempts to overthrow the DTO and return control to the people have failed. We must locate and rescue Travis at a time and place before they learn of it. That is our last hope for beating them."

Keene's mind spun. "Find Travis? They took him months ago. No one even knows where—"

"That's the problem." L's voice was grim. "We've searched every record. Nothing. In this timeline, it's as if he vanished off the face of the earth the day of the science competition in 2027...But we did find records on you."

Keene stiffened.

"In the original sequence of events, you died in that market shop we just came from. Shot in the storage we were just in. Which is how we knew where to find you before it happened."

Keene felt her knees weaken. The truth slammed into her—she should be dead. According to history anyways. She was only there because someone had meddled with the thread of time.

Her throat tightened. “So, what am I now? A ghost?”

“No,” L said firmly. “You’re alive. Which means you matter. Which means you have a choice. Follow me, we will continue our discussion over tea in a more comfortable setting. You must be tired from all the running and hiding your past few months...”

**Meanwhile, 2027 real time...**

The cell smelled of rot and iron. Travis sat hunched on his cot, staring at the dull pencil in his hand and the small, battered notebook on his lap.

He wasn’t supposed to have either.

They’d fallen out of a guard’s pocket weeks ago, when the man had rushed out after receiving what must have been an emergency call mid-shift. Travis had snatched them up and hidden them beneath his piss bucket, scrapping a hole into the floor with a wire from his cot until the concrete surrendered.

Now, when he was alone and no one was watching, he scribbled. Formulas. Theories.

Escape plans. Ideas he couldn't say out loud. Each line was survival—proof he was still thinking, still alive.

The notebook was his mind on paper, smuggled into the cracks of his prison.

But it was fragile. And if they ever found it—

Travis heard someone coming up the hall.

Quickly he tilted the half full bucket of his own waste and crammed the notebook and pencil into the indention he had made into the ground beneath it.

A small slosh as he dropped the bucket back into place.

Keys rattle.

The door clanged open.

Two guards, there to search him and escort him to the lab so that he can put the final touches on the new and improved quantum vision goggles.

Roughly they patted him down, as if they wanted to leave bruises. Handcuffs. An escort to the lab. Travis was used to his new routine.

But he still didn't like it.

**Hours later...**

Two guards dragged him back from the lab, tossing him into the cell like a sack of meat. Travis rolled to his knees, head pounding.

Another man lingered at the doorway, not a guard but someone higher, someone who watched with a predator's calm. His smile was wrong.

"So," the man drawled. "What side projects have you been working on, Travis?"

Travis blinked, trying to mask his fear. "I don't know what you mean."

"Oh...I think you do." The man stepped forward, his boots echoing. "You see Travis, nothing happens here without my knowledge. Not even, say...a guard losing his notebook and pencil in a very inconvenient place."

Travis's blood ran cold. His gaze betrayed him for a heartbeat, flicking toward the bucket. The realization washed over him that he had been played. He sat there, horrified and ashamed of his new predicament.

The man's smile widened. "So then, let's just see what kind of *shit* you've been up to."

With a swift kick, he sent the bucket flying. The warm splash of filth across Travis's chest hit first, then came the stench. Travis gagged, scrambling back against the wall.

The man stooped, lifted the stained notebook from its hiding place. He thumbed through the pages, eyes scanning the coded scrawl.

"Well, well," he murmured. "Now what's all this?"

Travis forced his face blank. "They're just formulas. Failed runs. Things that didn't work."

The man looked up slowly, his smile gone, replaced by something colder.

"Is that so?"

He closed the notebook with a snap, his eyes never leaving Travis.

"Come on now Travis. You don't really expect me to believe that do you? Should we check in and see how your little sister is these days?"

Travis's heart seized. His breath caught in his throat. And the cell suddenly felt smaller than ever.

## Chapter 14: Secrets by the Shore

**April 22nd, 2042, Cocoa Beach Florida**

The sand was deep beneath Alex's sneakers, the night breeze thick with salt and the faint smell of fried food drifting from the boardwalk. Cocoa Beach glowed with neon and laughter in the distance, but here, on the quieter stretch of shore, beneath the pier, the waves crashed against the darkness.

Alex stood with his hands shoved in his pockets, heart thumping hard. He'd told his classmates he needed fresh air, that he was going for a walk on the beach, and he'd be back before lights-out. Nobody asked questions. Nobody knew the weight in his chest.

Then she appeared.

Dr. Keene's hair streaked with gray, her face drawn and sharp. She walked with purpose, her shoes crunching against the shells, her eyes never leaving him.

"Why?" she asked.

Alex blinked. "Why what?"

“Why were you looking at the grassy knoll?” Her voice was low, cutting. “While every other student’s eyes were either on Kennedy, or Oswald’s window — you kept looking back. Again and again. Why?”

Alex’s mouth went dry. “I—I don’t know what you’re talking about.”

Keene’s gaze didn’t waver. “You’re lying. And you’re not very good at it. If I could see it, so did they.”

His chest tightened. “I don’t—”

“Alex.” Her tone softened slightly, but only slightly. “I’m not your enemy. I can’t tell you everything right now, but you need to understand something. If you saw, if you know something you aren’t supposed to — it matters. It puts you in danger. And others could be in danger as well.”

He looked at her, torn between fear and relief. She knew. She understood. But could he trust her?

Keene took a step closer. “If you keep this to yourself, they will find out anyway. The DTO always finds out. And when they do, they won’t just come for you. They’ll come for everyone involved. By then, it will be too late for us to help you."

Silence stretched between them, broken only by the surf.

Finally, Alex let out a shaky breath. "Okay. Okay, I'll tell you."

And he did.

The words tumbled out in a rush — how he smuggled the goggles past the guards, how he and his friends had tested them at Cowboy Stadium, how they'd laughed and partied, how none of them realized the risk. And then, finally, the secret he'd carried alone: slipping away to Dealey Plaza, dialing the goggles, and seeing what no one else had.

The bluer, brighter, more electric shimmery circle. The one the agent with the rifle came out of. The shot that didn't come from Oswald's window.

By the end his throat was raw, his hands trembling.

Keene closed her eyes briefly, as if bracing herself. "Just as I feared," she whispered.

Alex frowned. "But my friends—they didn't see anything. They were just messing around. It was only me."

"It doesn't matter," Keene said firmly. "If the DTO even suspects, they'll clean the slate. All of it. Anyone who might have seen something, even by accident. That's how they work. And that's why you can't go back."

Panic spiked in Alex's chest. "What do you mean, can't go back? My class is at the hotel—"

"You have to come with me now," Keene said, her voice steel. "We'll find a way to protect your friends, but you can't save them by staying in the open. The DTO is already watching you. If we don't move, you'll all be dead by sunrise."

Alex's pulse pounded in his ears. "What do you want from me?"

Keene's eyes bored into his. "There's work to do. And you're part of it now."

She lifted her hand, pressed something on the ring she was wearing on her middle right ring finger, and the air shimmered. A circle of light flared to life between them, rippling like water caught in the sun.

Alex's breath caught. He'd seen it once before — in Dealey Plaza, when the agent stepped through.

A portal.

Keene extended her hand. "Trust me, Alex. Step through."

Every instinct screamed at him to run. But somewhere deeper, curiosity, anger, and fear tangled into resolve.

He reached out, clasped her hand, and together they stepped into the light.

The portal sealed shut behind them with a whisper, leaving only the dark empty beach and the endless waves.

## Chapter 15: The Clones of History

A knock rattled the thin hotel door.

Noah groaned, dragging himself up from bed, still half-asleep. "Who the hell—"

He cracked it open. Two DTO agents filled the hallway, broad-shouldered, identical in their severity. Their dark jackets gleamed, their mirrored sunglasses reflecting Noah's pale face.

"Alexander James Wright," one said flatly. Not a question.

Noah blinked. "Alex? Uh...he's not here. Went for a walk on the beach. Hasn't come back yet."

The agents exchanged no words. One extended a gloved hand. "Goggles."

Noah hesitated. "What? No, those are for—"

The agent's grip tightened on the doorframe. His tone sharpened, the syllables like steel. "Now."

Noah scrambled back, fumbling with the cases on the desk. His fingers shook as he handed them over.

“And the ones assigned to Alexander James Wright.”

Noah walked over to Alex’s side of the room to retrieve them off his desk.

He walked back and handed them over.

“What’s this about?” he asked as the agent’s hands grasped the second case.

Without another word, the agents turned and strode down the hall, their boots heavy but silent against the carpet.

Noah stood frozen in the doorway, clutching the frame. The hallway seemed to close in, silent and endless.

He had no idea what was happening. Only that it was bad.

Very, very bad.

The portal snapped shut behind Alex with a shimmer.

He staggered, his knees weak, his head spinning as he looked around.

This wasn’t Cocoa Beach anymore.

The chamber was vast, carved from steel and humming with energy. Strange machines pulsed with blue light, cables snaked along the floors, and banks of monitors projected data in alien like symbols. People in gray uniforms moved briskly from station to station.

A tall woman stood waiting for them. Her hair was silver, her bearing calm but commanding. Her presence filled the room like a weight.

"Welcome back," she said, her voice steady. Her gaze shifted to Alex. "I see it was necessary to bring the boy after all."

Dr. Keene exhaled, tension still etched on her face. "He saw too much. More than he realizes. And the DTO is already circling him. Some of his classmates may be in danger also."

The woman nodded. Then she stepped closer, her sharp eyes pinning Alex in place.

"I am L," she said. "Leader of this rebel outpost. You are in danger, Alex. More danger than you understand."

Alex swallowed hard, his voice hoarse. "Because of the assassination? Because I saw--"

"Because the DTO has already seen you," L interrupted. "Every set of goggles records its use. At the end of every history tour, those logs are reviewed. They know where you looked. What you searched. How long your gaze lingered. Alex, they see exactly what you saw. If they are suspicious already that you've viewed outside the parameters of the approved curriculum, they will not wait until the tour ends. They will come now."

Alex's stomach sank. "But my friends—they didn't see anything! It was just me."

"It doesn't matter," L said. Her expression was unflinching. "The DTO will see the presence of your friends at unsanctioned views. They will assume everyone involved shares the same knowledge. Anyone who even might be privy to your secret will be silenced. That is how the DTO works. That is how they maintain control."

Her words landed like stones.

Alex's fists clenched. "So what do we do?"

L studied him for a long time. Then she asked: "The night you smuggled the goggles out. Who was with you? I need names. Their room assignments. Everything."

Alex hesitated. The thought of betraying his friends made bile rise in his throat. But then he considered what might happen to them if what L was saying is true.

If he didn't help, his friends were already dead.

He gave her the names. The details. Every word had him shifting between feelings of betrayal and that of relief.

L nodded once, filing it away without reaction.

"Good," she said. "Now since you have shown trust in me, I will do the same. Let me fill you in on what we know to be true."

She motioned to the machines, the glowing arcs of light around them. "This is the year 2183. As far as we know, we are the last rebel base standing."

Travis interrupted. "I'm sorry...did you say this was the year 2183?"

L continued.

"Travis—the man who created the goggles—discovered more than anyone realized. In 2027, he unlocked the secret for not only viewing the past, but stepping through it. A time portal. The

DTO kept it secret. They weaponized it. For decades, the world never even knew time travel existed. It was one of the many reasons the government kept such tight possession of the goggles and all notes and designs of said goggles. That and so they could rewrite history to their narrative without fear of resistance. Not until 2092, an event so catastrophic broke the façade, when the DTO's true intentions were revealed. Thousands of them appeared from the shadows taking out most of the population and the survivors learned the truth. By then it was too late. The DTO had already cemented power. The only choice left for those of us that remained was to hide."

Alex felt dizzy. His thoughts spun like a carousel. "DTO agents...all those men, all over the place. How do they—how are there so many?"

L's lips thinned. "Because they are the same man."

"What?"

"Clones," she said simply. "An elite soldier. Perfect at blending in, at surviving, at killing. They replicated him into an army. That is the DTO's shadow. Eyes everywhere at once. All linked telepathically as if they shared a single mind. Always the same face. Controlled by what was once our own government."

Alex's skin crawled. He thought of the agents at the hotel, their mirrored glasses, their identical movements.

"And what about the goggles?" he asked. "How—how does the portal work?"

"They are capable of more than you know," L said. "But the feature is hidden. Locked by code. A digital switch buried in the system. When enabled, the goggles can tear open a hole in space-time. But they cannot pass through their own portals. Matter cannot pass through energy that it is creating. To step across, you must leave the goggles behind. To return you need a second remote key."

She raised her hand. A small ring glinted on her finger. Silver, etched with faint lines of circuitry.

"This is the failsafe," she said. "A quantum remote, individually coded to each pair goggles. It signals them to open a portal five feet in front of the ring wearer as long as the paired goggles are still functional. With this, one may come and go. Without it...you could step through and never return."

Alex stared at it, awe and fear colliding in his chest as he realized he had already stepped through a portal without one. He had to trust them now. He was at their mercy.

L closed her hand over the ring. "That is why the DTO hunts us. That is why Travis must be found. And that is why you and your friends are now in this fight Alex."

She turned to a group of gray-uniformed operatives.

"Prepare a team," L ordered. "Retrieve these students from Cocoa Beach. Secure them before the DTO does."

The operatives saluted sharply and dispersed.

Alex's heart pounded as he watched them go.

He had dragged his friends into this. Now their lives hung in the balance.

And for the first time, he understood: there was no going back. Class was over. School was out.

## Chapter 16: Portals and Shadows

The hum of the machine filled the DTO's makeshift command center at the Cocoa Beach hotel. Agents in dark jackets hooked the goggles assigned to Noah into a sleek console. Wires spread across the desk like veins.

"Begin scan," one of the agents ordered.

Green light flickered across the goggles. Lines of code scrolled on the monitor.

"Nothing," a technician muttered. "Surface checks are clean. No anomalous searches."

The technician shook his head. "This one's empty."

"Move to the second set of goggles," the agent said.

Noah sat waiting on the edge of his bed, fear and confusion twisting together. He wanted to know what was happening, why had they taken their goggles, was it because Alex had smuggled his out? Deep down he knew it was. Where was Alex? How much trouble were they in? Mind racing in every direction. Not knowing what to do. If there was even anything he could do.

At that same moment, a shimmer of blue light rippled in the dark.

Two rebels stepped out and stood a few feet from Noah. His eyes widened, his jaw dropped. Unable to fathom what he had just witnessed.

“We were sent by Alex, you need to come with us.”

Noah was unsure if he should go with them. Concerned with what fate awaited him through the portal. However, the events of the evening had him calculating that his odds were better on the other side of whatever he was seeing than they were where he sat now. Cautiously, but willingly he stood up and followed them back into the portal.

A portal opened in the middle of another cramped dorm-style room. Two rebel operatives stepped out, sleek rifles slung across their backs.

The student sleeping there—Brian, the Cowboys fan—bolted upright in bed, his eyes wide. Convinced he was dreaming.

"What the hell—?!"

"We're here to help," one operative said firmly. "You need to come with us. Now."

Brian's mouth opened, then closed. His eyes darted to the portal, the humming circle of impossible energy in the middle of his room.

"You're—you're serious."

"Alex is already with us. We don't have time." the second operative snapped.

Brian swung his legs off the bed, "I ain't going nowhere until someone tells m..."

Before he could finish his sentence the rebels bound and gagged him. Then drug him through the portal as he thrashed and kicked in anger.

They vanished together through the light.

In another room, Maya sat at her desk scribbling in her journal when her mirror rippled, glowing blue. She dropped her pen with a gasp. The chair fell backwards as she sprang up.

A woman stepped out of the glass, followed closely by a rebel soldier.

"Don't scream," she said quickly. "You're not safe here. Alex sent us. The DTO will be coming for you soon. Take my hand."

Maya's heart pounded. "This... this isn't real."

"I assure you it is. And if you don't trust me, you'll be dead before morning."

Maya hesitated only a second longer before she reached out, trembling.

The portal sealed shut behind them.

Each reaction was catalogued, calmed, and met with firm reassurance.

But one room was empty.

Katie's.

Katie had finally convinced Tricia to go do something outside of school assignments. Tricia, reluctant as always, only agreed when Katie promised it would just be the two of them and they'd leave whenever Tricia wanted.

"Target not found," the rebel operatives reported.

Up the street, in a dim bar with sticky floors and the smell of saltwater beer, two students nursed cheap drinks. Katie & Tricia, oblivious to the storm brewing around them. They clinked glasses, laughed too loud, unaware that death had already been ordered for one of them.

Back in the DTO command center, the scan on Alex's goggles began to crawl across the screen.

The agent leaned in. "Pull the logs. Full report."

Lines of time-stamped data flickered past. Then froze.

A red alert blinked on the screen.

The technician's voice cracked. "Multiple unauthorized uses logged. One of those was November 22nd, 1963. Dealey Plaza. Extended view: grassy knoll. Duration: two minutes, twelve seconds."

The room went still.

“Playback confirms subject Alex Wright observed restricted event data,” the technician added. His face had gone white.

The lead agent pressed his earpiece. “Control, we have confirmation. Subject Wright accessed unsanctioned node, four other students possibly present or have knowledge of C.H.”

C.H. was code for ‘Classified History.’

Static. Then a new voice cut in, colder than the Atlantic breeze outside.

“Locate all involved students. Find out what they know and who they’ve talked to. Then terminate everyone involved. Immediate execution. No witnesses.”

The agents exchanged glances. No hesitation, no questions. Orders were orders.

“Understood.”

“Bravo team go.”

One by one the rooms were checked.

Bravo team squad leader pulled out his radio

“Sir… their rooms are empty. All of them.”

The Superior’s jaw tightened. “Empty?”

"Yes, sir. They're gone."

His voice angrier and much more commanding.

"Then find them. Now!"

## Chapter 17: Error Codes

The portals snapped shut behind them with a hiss of displaced air. Noah stumbled first, clutching his chest like he'd just been spun off a carnival ride. Maya doubled over, gagging, while Brian let out a string of curses that echoed off the steel walls of the rebel outpost as the gag was removed and he was released from the soldier's grasp. He calmed some when he finally noticed the others standing around him.

Alex was already there waiting, flanked by Dr. Keene and L. The air smelled faintly of ozone, machinery humming somewhere deep in the compound.

"Welcome to 2183," L said, her voice steady but brisk. "Take a moment. Breathe. You're safe here... for now."

"2183? Safe?" Brian barked. "We just went through a—through a—whatever that thing was! Where the hell are we? What's going on?"

Maya's head began to swim. She sat down hard, staring wide-eyed at the glowing console across the room. "Time travel isn't real. It's not real."

"It's very real," Keene said quietly. Her face softened. "And you've been brought here because you saw things that weren't sanctioned by the DTO. You were with Alex the night he smuggled the goggles out, weren't you?"

All three students froze.

Noah crossed his arms. "So what? We screwed around with history goggles. Big deal."

L stepped closer, her presence commanding. "The Department of Temporal Oversight does not see it as 'screwing around.' They see liabilities. Liabilities are erased."

Brian's anger faltered. "Erased... you mean—"

"Dead," Keene finished. "And if we hadn't pulled you out tonight, you'd already be listed in the obituaries."

The three exchanged looks, a cocktail of disbelief and dread.

Maya was the first to speak. "Where's Katie? She was with us that night! Is she okay?"

“We have a team ready to extract her and her friend, one Tricia Barton. They are currently in a heavily populated area.”

“Tricia wasn’t with us that night,” Noah said. “She’s not part of any of this.”

L stepped forward. “That may be but our records indicate that both their bodies were found dead in the alley beside The Blue Oyster club, mugging turned deadly according to police reports. We are now researching all available records to find a secure extraction point and time. That’s the strange thing about time travel, as long as you can survive the present you can always do something about the past.”

“Shit.” Was all Brian could muster.

L responded, “That’s what we are telling all of you, you are in serious...shit. Because of what Alex did. What he saw and what he now knows to be true.”

Alex shifted uneasily, hands in his pockets, like he was both inside the circle and apart from it. Then L turned to him.

“Go on. Tell them.”

Alex swallowed. "Right. So... uh... the night before the official JFK viewing, when I had snuck the goggles out. I kind of wandered off on my own to stay out a little longer when y'all went upstairs."

Noah stared. "You what?"

Alex raised his hand. "Look, I know it was stupid, okay? I just wanted to see it first without all the DTO breathing down our necks."

He paused, his throat dry. "Only... what I saw wasn't what we were shown the next day. There was this... portal. Out of nowhere. And a DTO agent stepped through. He's the one who fired the shot that killed President Kennedy. Oswald saw him too—tried to stop him—but the agent just stepped back through and disappeared."

Maya's face drained of color. "You're saying—"

"That the assassination we've been taught our whole lives is a cover," Alex said. "The DTO controls history."

Silence fell like a hammer.

Brian rubbed his temples. "This is insane. Absolutely insane."

L crossed her arms. “And yet, here you are. You’ve seen too much. Which is why you need to understand the stakes.”

The questions all came at once. Who are you really? Why us? How long has this been going on?

L held up her hand. “One at a time.” She took a breath. “I wasn’t always part of this rebellion. I was brought in... adopted, if you will... in the year 2123, three years after the rebellion had obtained Travis Calder’s notes and was able to decipher them to unlock the time travel function on the goggles. For nearly a hundred years, the DTO had the only knowledge and capability of time travel, giving them complete control. We have been searching for Travis ever since we cracked it ourselves, sixty years, trying to find a place and time he is being held that we can rescue him from.”

Brian blinked like he was malfunctioning trying to keep up with all the information he was receiving.

L continued, “As for the goggles: we have scoured their code. Every line Travis wrote. Every annotation. We’ve checked every notebook that we know was his and a few we just suspected could have been. Every scrap. But we cannot find where he was taken all those years ago. The only leads we ever had were some error codes. When we ran it through deep analysis, it translated into what looked like a date and time...we even found coordinates but let's just say, those were a dead end."

Alex's face lit up. "Wait. You mean like the error code you get when you set your goggles to the future?"

L blinked at him, caught off guard. Then—just barely—she smiled. "Sharp boy."

"Sharpest in Alabama," Alex said, puffing out his chest. "Roll Tide."

Keene shot him a look sharp enough to cut steel. Perhaps just out of reflex from having been a professor at LSU. Regardless, the look told Alex this was neither the time or place for school spirit.

"...Sorry," Alex muttered.

L continued. "Plus, if we've found the information then surely the DTO has as well which is probably why it's misleading. There must be another hidden code. Something we've overlooked. But we've exhausted every avenue we can think of. Every GPS coordinate we've found has led us to a dangerous encounter."

**Meanwhile, in 2027.**

Travis sat shackled in the same interrogation room he had been months ago. Where he watched his friend get killed and drug away. His lips were split, his body bruised, his mind ragged but unbroken.

The interrogator paced, notebook in hand. Pages filled with Travis's equations and half-coded sequences.

'Formulas and codes that didn't work,' Travis had said.

The man slammed the notebook on the table. "You really think you can play me? You will give us what we want."

Travis stayed silent, jaw set.

The man leaned in close. "Remember Travis, we know where your sister is. Lydia. Sweet girl, been through so much already. Lost her parents. Her brother vanished, assumed to be one of the unidentifiable bodies from the campus tragedy, leaving her stranded in foster care. It would be a shame if she had an accident or decided to run away never to be heard from again. I had a feeling you may be hesitant to cooperate. I've already dispatched men to her foster home to see how she's adjusting to her new life."

Travis's stomach dropped, but he kept his face hard. He couldn't give them what they wanted. Millions of others could be harmed. That he knew. He wouldn't. He couldn't. This was bigger than one person, even if it was the last person alive that Travis truly cared about. But he needed time. Also, he had a feeling. Deep down. A feeling that his sister was safe. Or a 'hope' that she was. Hope was something he had given up for himself months earlier, but he still had plenty for Lydia. She was safe. He couldn't explain it. But he felt it nonetheless.

"Show me," he said finally, his voice rough. "Show me proof she's alive. Swear you won't harm her. Then I'll cooperate. Then and only then, I'll tell you whatever the fuck you want to know."

The interrogator narrowed his eyes. The room stretched with silence. Finally, he snapped his fingers at one of the guards. "Very well."

They waited. Seconds dragged into minutes.

At last, an agent entered and leaned close, whispering in the interrogator's ear.

The man's expression flickered—anger barely contained. He straightened, smoothing his tie.

Travis fought back a grin.

"It appears," he said slowly, "that we are... having trouble locating her at this precise moment. But rest assured. We will."

For the first time since his capture, Travis smiled. A small, defiant smirk. He didn't even try to hide it. He wore it proudly as he locked eyes with the interrogator.

"Well then," he said, "for now it looks like you've lost your leverage. Because I'm not telling you anything until I know she's safe and I seriously doubt you'll ever find her. Without proof of my sister's safety, there isn't a damn thing you can do to make me give you asshats the answers you want."

The interrogator's face flushed crimson. He slammed the table and barked at the guards. "Take him back! Throw him in his cell and lock it down. Complete sensory deprivation until I say otherwise. Let's see how long you last with only your thoughts and fears to keep you company Mr. Calder."

They dragged Travis down the corridor and flung him into his cell.

As he staggered inside, his eyes caught a glimpse of a guard's wristwatch in the scuffle.

1:51 PM.

9-10-27.

As Travis stood there watching the guards walk away, he heard the man that had been interrogating him yelling from the other side of the door at the end of the hall, "I don't care what you have to do, find the girl before I have to report to the Superior!"

The lights went out; panels came down over the door and windows blocking any sound or light from getting in.

Travis sat down on the cot, dripping sweat and blood, but smiling faintly.

He finally had something. Hope. For Lydia and himself. Faint, but there.

## Chapter 18: Close Calls

**2042 Cocoa Beach Florida.**

The Florida night air was thick, heavy with the stink of diesel and rain.

DTO agents fanned out across the streets, their identical faces grim under the glow of sodium lamps. Radios crackled with clipped commands.

“Target subjects not in their quarters. Sweep perimeter.”

“Copy. Moving north along Commerce.”

Unaware that most of their quarry were already gone, the agents moved with precision. Only one loose thread remained at risk.

Katie.

Her and Tricia emerged from the dim bar, laughter clinging to their voices, dulled by cheap whiskey. Katie tugged her jacket tighter against the wind, her cheeks flushed. Tricia hummed under her breath, heels clicking against the cracked pavement.

“Should we get an Uber?” Tricia asked.

"It's a nice night for a walk now that the rain is gone. And the room's not that far up ahead," Katie said, pointing down the block.

Neither noticed the agent across the street. His eyes narrowed, recognition sparking. He raised his radio. Reported the sighting. Then started across the street towards the girls. Flanking them from behind.

"Control, this is Unit Seven. I have visual on Subject Katie—"

He didn't finish.

A low hum rippled from the alley beside them, vibrating in their bones. Katie stopped dead, her head snapping toward the sound.

A portal ripped open, light spilling like liquid fire.

"What the—?" Tricia gasped.

Figures leapt through—armed, fast, clad in rebel insignia. Before Katie could move, rough hands grabbed her, pulling her backward. Tricia screamed, thrashing, until another rebel seized her by the waist.

"No! Let me go! Help!"

Katie just screamed.

The DTO agent broke into a sprint, boots hammering pavement. He raised his pistol, muzzle flashing in the dark. Bullets sparked against the bricks.

"Move! Stop fighting us!" a rebel barked, dragging the girls deeper into the light.

Katie's vision fractured, caught between two worlds—Florida night shrinking behind her, searing brilliance ahead.

The last thing she saw was the DTO agent lunging, arm outstretched, fingertips inches from the portal's edge.

Then—nothing.

The portal snapped shut, the night silent once more.

The agent slammed his fist into the wall, teeth bared. He grabbed his radio, voice sharp.

"Control. There may be a problem."

**2027 Sensory Deprivation, Day 3/Travis Calder's Cell.**

Travis sat in his cell, the dark filled the room. The stink of piss and shit from the overturned bucket still lingered.

He stared into the darknessl, mind racing.

They'd lost Lydia. He knew it from the fury in the interrogator's eyes. Which meant they no longer had leverage. Which meant his only weapon was time. They had just armed him with 3 days. He had a plan. He had long ago figured out the geographic coordinates of where he was being held. He had seen a date and time a few days prior. Now he just needed a way to get the information to someone that would and could help.

If he could get back into the lab—if he could install some back doors, program some fail-safes, slip in the right line of code, disguised as junk or failed equations—then maybe, just maybe, someone in the future could find him.

But his captors were watching him closer now. Any sudden diligence would smell of desperation. He had to play dumb, be defiant, until they gave him an excuse to act broken and cave in to their demands.

He let out a bitter laugh as he whispered to himself. “Coy, Travis. You’ve gotta play it coy.”

The words echoed back at him from the walls, hollow and thin.

He lay down on the cot, staring towards the plate of steel blocking his usual small view of the stars. Total darkness. In his head, numbers and lines of code unraveled, rewove, coiled themselves into a hidden key.

He only needed one more chance.

**2183 Rebel Base.**

The rebel outpost’s air was electric with tension. Alex, Noah, Brian, and Maya sat opposite Dr. Keene and L, their voices rising and falling in disbelief, frustration, and fear.

“This is insane,” Brian muttered for the tenth time. “We’re supposed to be on a history tour. Not... not fugitives.”

“We’re here because of Alex,” Maya shot back, glaring. “He’s the one who smuggled the goggles out. He's the one that looked where he wasn't supposed to."

"Hey," Alex bristled. "You were all laughing it up when we were not watching the Cowboys win their Super Bowl."

"This isn't a joke!" Maya snapped.

L's voice cut through the bickering. "Enough. Blame does not matter now. Survival does."

The room hummed. A portal opened against the far wall, blue light spilling like a wound in space.

Two rebels stumbled through, dragging Katie and Tricia with them.

Katie's eyes darted around the outpost, wide with terror and disbelief.

Tricia screamed. "Where are we? What did you do to us?!" She tore against her captors, hair wild, fists striking anything she could reach.

Katie froze as she spotted Alex. "Oh my God. Alex?"

Alex raised a hand weakly. "Hey. Uh... welcome to the future?"

Dr. Keene crossed the floor quickly. "Katie. Listen. You're safe here. But we need you to understand—"

Katie shook her head, trembling. "Safe? We were grabbed by strangers out of an alley—what the hell is happening?!"

Tricia's screams pitched higher, echoing off the steel walls. "I want out! Take me back! Take me back right now!"

Two rebels tried to restrain her. She kicked, clawed, spat.

"Damn it," L muttered. She reached into her coat and withdrew a slim injector.

Tricia froze for half a second as the needle touched her arm. Then her knees buckled. She slumped, unconscious, into the rebels' arms.

Katie gasped. "What did you do to her?"

"Tranquilizer," L said calmly. "For her safety—and ours. Take her to the infirmary."

Two rebel soldiers drug her away at the command.

Katie stared at Tricia's limp body as they exited the chamber, then at the faces around her—Alex, her classmates, these strangers in the future.

She swallowed hard, the walls of reality crashing in.

## Chapter 19: Codes and Shadows

**2027**

Travis's cell door screeched open. Two guards stepped in, rifles raised.

"On your feet," one barked.

Travis sat still on the cot, staring at the floor. His jaw clenched, knuckles white.

"Not today. Not until you can prove my sister is okay. So go eat a dick."

The butt of a rifle cracked against his ribs, folding him over with a grunt. Hands grabbed him, yanking him to his feet. They dragged him down the hall, his bare feet slapping concrete, every joint screaming from weeks of torture.

The door to the lab opened. Fluorescent light stabbed his eyes. The interrogator—the same man with the dead stare—waited at the workstation.

"You've stalled long enough, Travis." His voice was smooth, rehearsed. "We know what you and your goggles are capable of. So, you're going to confirm what we already know and get back to work to make it happen."

Travis coughed blood onto the floor. "And if I don't?"

The man gave a thin smile and slid a folder across the desk. Inside were reconnaissance photos—grainy images of a skyline, a football stadium packed with people, a children's hospital.

"We may not be able to find your sister, but we don't need her anymore," the man said coldly. "If you won't cooperate, we'll collapse a city block. One each day until you give us what we want. These are potential targets. Thousands dead. Entirely your fault. Do you really want that on your conscience?"

Travis's throat tightened. "You're bluffing."

The man leaned closer. "Care to test me?"

Travis's hands trembled. They'd killed his parents. Miles. They'd nearly taken Lydia. He knew they'd carry through with their threats of killing thousands. He knew they weren't bluffing. He also knew that even more lives were at stake if they got what they wanted. But Travis also had a plan. And all he needed was an excuse to get behind the computer one more time.

They had just given it to him.

"You bastards," he whispered, playing the part of defeated victim. It was easy for him to do. He had felt it over and over again since the day he had been taken. "You'll never win."

But when they shoved him into the chair and powered on the terminal, his fingers flew over the keys. Line after line of code poured onto the screen, sweat dripping down his temple.

Not just refinements for their goggles—buried deep in the syntax was his secret. A signature. An error message. A hidden key. A key to his salvation.

Every keystroke was rebellion.

**2042.**

In Washington DC, the DTO headquarters buzzed with agitation. The head agent stood before his superior, boots planted firmly, jaw set.

"They slipped through our hands, sir. Two of the girls. Pulled into portals by someone before we could intercept. We're still searching, but it's safe to assume the others have already been recovered by the same people as well."

The superior—a tall man with black iron-gray streaked hair and a small mustache—listened in silence, fingers steepled under his chin.

"An independent group knows much more about time travel than they should, somewhere in the future there has been an information leak," the agent pressed. "And our inability to breach the future cripples us. We can chase shadows of the past all we want, but they're coming for us from the other side."

The superior rose from his chair slowly. His voice was calm, almost soothing.

"I understand your concerns. Leave them to me."

The agent hesitated, then saluted sharply. "Yes, sir."

The door shut, leaving the superior alone in the dim office.

For a long moment, he stood motionless. Then his hand slipped into his pocket and closed around a simple silver band. He lifted it, pressed the recessed stud.

A portal blossomed before him, light spilling across the room. He stepped forward without hesitation.

When the brightness faded, he stood beneath a darkened sky of towering glass spires. Neon burned against black steel. The skyline of 2215. Not his time of origin, but a point in time he had been to once before.

The Masters had brought him here when they first recruited him. His task: build the DTO stronger, control their narrative of history, ensure that the people never reclaimed power or learned of the ability to time travel.  In exchange he was given charge over the DTO and time itself which more than quenched his thirst for power. His lifestyle had become more lavish than he could have imagined.  He lived as he believed royalty would.

His mission had been a success. Until now.

## Chapter 20: Masters of 2215

The city of New York 2215 stretched out in neon veins and black steel arteries. Skyscrapers like needles stabbed at the sky, their windows pulsing with digital life. Hovercraft hummed above, while the streets far below glowed with symbols projected into the air—language that had evolved quite a deal since the Superior's time.

He stood on a high balcony of the Citadel, the fortress at the city's heart looking out. Even now, with everything he had seen, decades after he'd departed for his mission in the early 2000s, the sheer size of it still left him uneasy. When he'd first left, this city had been different—less refined, more fractured. But his work in reshaping history had borne fruit. He had given his Masters a better world.

At least... that was the story he told himself.

Inside, the chamber pulsed with cold light. Six figures sat in massive chairs, their faces hidden in shadow behind glass screens. Their voices carried in unison, electronically layered so that even one whisper rattled like thunder.

"You have returned," they said in unison.

"Yes, Masters." The Superior bowed. "The DTO is thriving in 2042. History remains... contained."

"Contained," one of the voices hissed. "But unstable."

The screens flickered, displaying maps—continents fractured, oceans swelling, fault lines glowing. Images of tsunamis, hurricanes, earthquakes, raging wildfires.

"These events were not in our records," the Masters said. "Natural disasters on scales unseen. Evidence the past is shifting again."

The Superior straightened, jaw tight. "Impossible. We have locked it down. We control the technology. No one can alter unless we permit."

"Then explain this," a Master said. The screen behind him shifted, showing a rebel stronghold burning, bodies on the ground. And one prisoner bound to a chair under bright interrogation lights.

A man with weathered skin and graying hair.

"This one spoke before he died," the Masters intoned. "He claimed the rebels unlocked the ability to time travel in 2123. He also claimed to be from 2042, one of the years in the time you were charged with policing. We gave you dominance and excessive resources to do so. We only asked that you prioritize protecting our interest. The prisoner claims he has been under the protection of these rebels since the year 2183. Are we to believe that he has lived a fugitive of your time dominion these past 32 years without your knowledge? That you knew and did nothing? Or that you sanctioned an obviously flawed mission? None speak highly of your leadership skills."

The Superior stepped closer, his heart pounding. Half of him embarrassed, the other part was angry. "Who is this prisoner?"

"His name," the Masters said, "is Noah."

The Superior froze.

That was one of the names of Alex's group. Of one of the students missing from the 2042 history trip.

But this Noah was older—his face lined, his voice hoarse but defiant even as they played the recording of his interrogation:

"You can keep your lies. You can rewrite your history a thousand times, but truth doesn't die. We know. Alex saw what you did. He knows you're all frauds. And if I'm here, then it means he and the others made it out. You can't erase us all."

The screen cut back to static. The Masters leaned forward, shadows warping.

"You see," they said. "Your grip on history is failing. The rebels shelter these students in 2183. Find them. Eradicate them. Restore the timeline. If we must handle the situation, we will also have to evaluate your current position."

The Superior bowed low, though his mind was reeling.

If Noah had survived into this future, if Alex and the others were truly in 2183, then his mission wasn't just preservation anymore. It was in jeopardy. It was war.

## Chapter 21: Theories and Hunters

**2183.**

The common room in the rebels' compound was lit by low, humming lamps. Screens flickered with schematics of goggles, portal rings, and strands of code that looked more like abstract art than technology.

Brian leaned forward on the table, eyes narrowed. "So you're telling me they've been trying to find this Travis guy for over a century?"

Maya crossed her arms. "Think about it. If he was the one who invented the goggles and discovered time travel, he'd have to know they'd try to bury him forever. He must've left something behind. Something somewhere nobody would think to look."

Noah tapped his fingers restlessly. "It's gotta be already hidden inside the goggles, waiting for someone to stumble on it. That's the only thing he'd ever be able to get out so it only makes sense."

Katie frowned. "Let's go over what we know. We've been told about the restrictions a dozen times. You can't use them to look into the future. They can't go through the portals they make. And the rings are just... keys. Without them, you're stuck.  All the error codes have been found, L said they lead to dangerous places with no sign of Travis."

For a long moment, silence. Just the buzz of the lamps and the faint thrum of distant generators.

Then Alex shot upright, eyes wide. "Wait—wait, wait, wait!" He grabbed his hair like it might slip away if he didn't hold onto it. "I think I got it—I think I got it!"

Everyone turned to stare.

"Got what?" Brian asked, annoyed.

Alex didn't answer. He bolted to his feet. "I need Keene. And L. Right now."

"Alex—what are you talking about?" Maya demanded.

But he was already out the door, footsteps echoing down the corridor, leaving the others in a swirl of confusion.

Maya looked around at the group still gathered at the table. "Does... does anyone else feel like we're always two steps behind him?"

Noah sighed. "Welcome to my life."

Katie just rolled her eyes, "I'm going to go check on Tricia."

**2042.**

The Superior stood in a sealed hangar, his face lit only by the glow of floodlights. Ten DTO soldiers knelt before him, identical in stance and sharpness. They wore black combat gear, their rings glinting faintly at their sides.

"You will not ask why," the Superior intoned. "You will not ask where. You will act. And you will destroy."

The agents didn't flinch.

"Our quarry believes themselves untouchable. Hidden. They are wrong. I have located them." His voice sharpened. "This time, you make no effort to disguise the kill. No staged accidents. No excuses. Leave none of them alive."

The Superior raised his hand. A portal rippled open behind him, swirling with pale blue light.

“Go,” he commanded.

The agents sprinted forward and disappeared into the portal.

The hangar fell silent again.

**2183**.

They emerged from the portal at the tree line of a forest, the skyline of 2183 cutting jagged against the stars.

The portal hissed closed behind them.

The agents turned, one by one, staring into the empty air. Confused as to why none of their digital equipment would work. No readings. No information as to date or location. One by one they tried activating a portal with their ring remotes. Nothing happened. Just the soft click of a button.

The squad leader clenched his jaw, scanning the alien skyline. “We’re not in 2042 anymore. Somehow, we have been sent forward from our present.”

Confusion spread through the squad as they realized the truth: they had been thrown forward into the very future they were told was unreachable. No way home.

And their orders were clear.

Find the students. Kill them all. But then what? No way back. Succeed or fail...This was a suicide mission.

# Chapter 22: The Forbidden Rule

**2027**

Travis woke with a start on the thin cot, earlier than usual, unable to sleep. Heart hammering, from excitement instead of fear this time.

The cell was still dark, the faint hum of the lights outside his only marker that morning had come. He sat up slowly, forcing his hands to tremble, his shoulders to sag, his breaths to rasp. He needed them to see a broken man.

But inside, his mind raced.

Today is the day.

If he'd hidden it well enough—if the misdirection held, if someone out there figured it out—then today would be it. His rescue. His freedom.

Don't smile, he told himself. Don't show it. Just one more performance. The best one yet. Revenge.

The footsteps came. Heavy boots outside the door. Keys jingling.

The lock scraped, then the iron door screeched open. Two guards stepped inside, rifles at the ready.

"Up," one barked.

Travis groaned, forced himself to move sluggishly, as though every muscle ached. His wrists burned as the cuffs snapped on, but his pulse surged. Every step down the corridor was agony to fake, excitement buried under the mask of exhaustion.

They shoved him into the lab wing. His breath caught.

The lab wasn't empty today. Even better. An audience.

A dozen men and women in black suits stood waiting, faces grim, eyes sharp. He stopped in the doorway, chained, his stomach twisting with excitement.

He fought back a smile as he thought to himself-'Well the gang's all here, time for the show. Go big or go home.'

He stood, preparing himself to 'Go big.'

And still—part of him whispered—or maybe this is it.

**2183**

Katie kicked at the leaves on the path, her arms folded. Tricia walked beside her, eyes wide and restless, every sound in the woods making her flinch.

"This is insane," Tricia muttered for the hundredth time. "Portals? Government clones? Us being trapped in the future? I can't—my brain just doesn't—"

"That's why they're letting us walk," Katie said softly, glancing back at the chaperone rebel soldier trailing behind. "You've been losing it. Fresh air helps."

"It doesn't help that I feel like I'm in a cage even out here. It doesn't help me get home to my family. It doesn't help me get the degree I've been working for my whole life. And it really doesn't help my outlook for the future."

Katie sighed. "Yeah. I know."

The chaperone said nothing, watchful, his hand never straying far from the weapon at his side. The forest seemed peaceful, but even here secrecy was survival. No one was left alone. No one was unsupervised.  Not away from the safety of their secret living quarters anyway.

Meanwhile, Alex nearly skidded into the room where Dr. Keene and L were poring over projection screens filled with scrolling data.

"I've got it!" Alex blurted.

Both women looked up.

"Two ideas," he panted. "Based on the rules the goggles came with." He jabbed a finger toward the schematics on the screen. "First: you can't go into the future. If you try, you get an error code. That code—the one that looks like a date and time. Useless without a location though right?"

L and Keene exchanged a glance but let him continue.

"Second: the goggles can't make a portal where one already exists. The same energy can't exist in the same place twice. What if you tried it? Try to double-open? Maybe that's the code we're missing. *Maybe*, that's where we'll find Travis' location!"

He was grinning, alive with the discovery.

L and Keene shared another, more weighted glance. Then L said gently, "That's a brilliant idea, Alex. Truly."

"But," Keene added, "we've already tried that."

Alex froze.

"When you attempt to open a portal where one already exists, the goggles do indeed throw an error code of geographic coordinates," Keene explained. "30-41-02N, 91-18-57W. But when we followed the codes to that precise location at the exact date and time given in the other error message... we wound up in the tiger enclosure on the LSU campus. Face-to-face with Mike. Nearly lost an operative."

Alex blinked. Then, slowly, his smile returned.

"Booby trap," he whispered.

Keene frowned. "What?"

"Think about it!" Alex's voice rose, filled with excitement. "Travis knew they'd be looking for codes. He knew his captors would test everything he wrote, every limit he gave them. So he left easy ones for them to find. Decoys. Anyone could stumble onto them. Maybe even crack them. But they weren't meant for allies—they were meant to throw off the DTO or any other government agency behind his incarceration."

Keene's eyes widened slightly.

"He buried his information deeper," Alex said, practically vibrating with energy. "Past the fake rules. Past the safe tests. In the one warning he swore no one should ever break."

He leaned forward, voice dropping.

"Which brings us to my second idea. What if we do the one thing we're not supposed to? Defy the warning everyone repeats about the goggles—the one thing they say could unravel time and space itself?"

The room went still.

Keene stared at him like he'd lost his mind.

L's lips tightened, her eyes shadowed with something between fear and admiration.

Finally, Keene spoke, “I know you aren’t suggesting what I think you are.”

And Alex, flushed with certainty, whispered, “That’s how we’ll get the real codes and find where Travis is.”

## Chapter 23: Collision

**2183.**

The forest loomed around the DTO soldiers, unfamiliar and silent except for the drone of insects.

"Orders?" one asked, his voice clipped, mechanical.

The squad leader scanned the skyline in the distance, neon glows peeking through the tree line. "We don't know where—or when—we are. You seven are with me, we'll set up camp here within the tree line. You two go into town for reconnaissance. Observation only, then report back here by sunrise. Move."

The two split without hesitation, heading towards the neon lights in the distance. The squad leader spoke to the remaining seven agents, "We'll make camp just inside the tree line. You four drop packs and begin carving a perimeter and assembling shelters from field gear. You two head off in that direction, search for food, water, anything useful. You. You're with me, we'll go this way and do the same. Report back here within the hour."

The first pair of soldiers went walking northeast down a narrow trail that went deep into the trees. They hadn't gotten far into the forest when one of them spotted movement further up the path. A man and two young women.

The man carried a weapon. The women did not.

The DTO soldiers took cover, assessing the situation, then raised their rifles.

Peering through their scopes.

One whispered: "Target identified. Katie." The second responded, "I'll take out the armed escort, you take out the target, we'll capture the other for questioning."

A soft squeeze of the trigger—crack. The rebel chaperone stumbled, chest blooming red, then crumpled into the leaves.

The girls screamed. Katie grabbed Tricia's hand, pulling her as they ran. But the soldiers were faster, disciplined.

Another shot rang out. Katie jerked forward, then fell hard, face hitting the dirt. Blood spread across her back.

"NO!" Tricia dropped beside her, sobbing, trying to roll her over, to press down on the wound. "Stay with me—Katie, please—"

But Katie only let out a bloody cough, then a gargling sound. Her eyes went glassy, her chest still.

Tricia's scream ripped through the forest, raw and feral. "SOMEBODY HELP!"

The agents were on her in an instant, dragging her away from the body. Her fists flailed, her voice cracked with terror.

"LET ME GO! HELP!"

"Quiet," one snapped.

They bound her wrists, gagged her mouth, and hauled her back through the trees. Behind them, the rebel soldier struggled with his last breath trying to grasp his radio. Unsuccessfully. Movement ceased. He was gone. A few feet from him Katie's lifeless body lay sprawled in the dirt, her blood soaking into the roots.

**2027**

The lab was thick with silence as Travis stood before the row of suited men, every eye on him. His chains clinked softly as he gestured toward the diagrams and boards arrayed across the room.

"This," he began, voice steady, "is the foundation of the quantum vision goggles. A lens that doesn't just see light, but memory—quantum imprints of reality itself. With them, you can view the past as it unfolded. Like pressing play on the universe's recordings."

He paced, speaking with precision.

"But you cannot look forward. The future isn't there—not because the goggles fail, but because it's an incomplete story. You can't read the last page of a book that hasn't been written."

Some of the men scribbled notes, others leaned in, rapt.

"The past and the present however," Travis continued, "are stories of the book, written in pencil. They can be erased and rewritten. But the unwritten future? That's ink that hasn't touched the page."

He let the words hang for a moment.

"With additional coding and materials, the goggles can open a door, or portal rather, large enough for a person to pass through in the space time continuum to any point and time. The same rules apply here; you cannot travel forward to any point in time that you or your goggles didn't already exist because the pages of the story aren't there. When it comes to traveling through time rather than just viewing it, there are additional rules that apply."

Then he added, voice low and sharp: "And energy follows these rules. First rule is that the same energy cannot occupy the same space at the same moment. So, if you open a portal and someone else tries to open a portal there at the exact place and time, the goggles have a safe guard that won't allow it. So, two portals accidentally colliding is impossible. Now if you force two portals together—which is possible, but...I must insist you don't because, um..."

He stopped, staring at each of them in turn.

“Well—you’d create an explosion that wouldn’t just level a city. It would unravel time itself. Space. Reality. A reset of the entire universe. Everything gone.”

A ripple of shock passed through the room. Several men gasped. Others whispered to each other.

One finally leaned forward, eyes gleaming. “Show us what they can do that *is* allowed.”

“Yes,” another said, “demonstrations. We want proof of what this device can do.”

Travis lowered his head, hiding the curl of his lips.

‘I thought you’d never ask,’ he thought as he started twisting dials on the goggles.

## Chapter 24: Defiance

**2183**

The campfire burned low, casting jagged shadows across the DTO soldier's faces. Tricia sat bound to a post, her wrists raw, her eyes wide and tear streaked. Eight soldiers ringed the camp, silent but watchful, predators biding their time.

"Where are the others?" the squad leader demanded.

Tricia shook her head furiously. "I don't know. I don't know anything."

One of the agents sneered. He stepped forward, drew his field knife, and twirled it casually in his gloved hand. "We don't have time for this," he muttered to the other soldiers

He turned to Tricia and knelt until they were face to face. "I know you're lying. This is your last chance to answer the question."

"No—I swear—" Tricia started to say.

The knife flashed. A scream tore from her throat as the blade severed flesh and bone, her pointer finger dropping into the dirt.

She thrashed, sobbing uncontrollably, blood spilling onto her lap.

"All of it," the squad leader said coldly. "Now. You've got nine more I can cut off before I move to toes."

And Tricia broke.

She told them everything, or what little she knew. Through sobs of pain and fear. About Alex smuggling the goggles out on their educational history tour. About what he had seen in Dallas—the portal, the agent, the assassination. About the rebels who had pulled them into 2183. About Travis, lost in time, and their search to retrieve him. And finally, her voice shaking, she whispered the location of the hidden entrance to the rebel base.

The squad leader stood. "Two stay here with her. Wait for the recon man to return. The rest—on me. Move out."

Six soldiers melted into the forest, their rifles glinting faintly under the moonlight, heading straight for the rebels' sanctuary.

**Rebel Outpost – 2183**

Alex's eyes blazed as he leaned across the table. "It has to be this. Travis knew they'd test the easy limits. That's why he buried fake answers in the error codes. He wanted them to be distracted. But the one warning—the absolute do-not-touch rule? That's where he hid the real information."

L's expression was unreadable. Keene's brow furrowed.

Alex pressed on, his words tumbling over themselves. "Think about it—if they thought colliding two portals would unravel time and space, they'd never risk it. Total destruction benefits nobody. But Travis? He'd have safeguards. He wouldn't let the universe implode. He hid the truth where only the desperate—or the brave—would dare to look."

Keene folded her arms. "Or he meant what he said, Alex. And colliding portals really would destroy everyone and everything."

L tapped her fingers against her chin, studying him with unsettling calm. "It is bold. Dangerous. Perhaps insane."

"It's everything I've heard about Travis," Alex said. "What better middle finger to his captors than hiding his secret in the one place they'd never dare touch?"

The tension was broken by the sudden arrival of a rebel soldier, panting.

"Commander L," he gasped, "the escort hasn't checked in. No response to dispatch. We've been attempting to make contact with them for almost an hour."

L stiffened. "Assemble a search party. Eight soldiers, four teams of two. Sweep the woods."

The soldier nodded and ran.

Alex exchanged a look with Keene, both realizing at once: something was very, very wrong.

**2027**

The lab hummed with power as Travis adjusted the sleek new goggles. The men in suits leaned forward, every pair of eyes fixed on the display monitor synced to the goggles.

Travis dialed in a date. The screen flickered to show himself, days earlier, hunched over a workstation under the watchful eye of guards.

"Incredible," one of the men whispered.

He changed dates, times—flashing clips of himself working, being escorted, even dragged half-conscious back to his cell. Hoping the sight of his mistreatment would lead to his salvation from his current captors. The suits murmured among themselves, astonished by the capabilities of the goggles already. Noe of them seemed to notice or care about much else.

Then Travis let the goggles whir, made a final adjustment—and the air shimmered. A portal ripped open in the center of the lab, pulsing blue.

Gasps erupted. The men surged forward, awestruck. Reaching out but scared to touch it.

Travis raised his hand. "I could demonstrate stepping through..."

But the interrogator snapped, "Absolutely not Mr. Calder." He jabbed a finger at two guards. "You two. Go."

The men hesitated, exchanging glances of uncertainty, then obeyed, easing into the portal, then vanishing into the light. Travis pushed a button on the goggles. The portal closed behind them.

"Impressive Mr. Calder. Now open it again and bring them back," the interrogator ordered.

Travis cocked his head, locking eyes with his captor, stone faced. "Nah, I don't think I will."

The room went still.

"And to get themselves back they'll need a secondary device," Travis said smoothly. "A remote, synced to the goggles. Without it, they're stranded. And since I was never asked to make one of those—well...I didn't." He spread his hands.

Rage ignited in the interrogator's eyes. "Where did you send them?"

Travis's smirk was razor-thin. "History," he whispered patronizingly.

The interrogator seized his collar. “TELL ME!”

Travis leaned close, eyes glittering. “Let’s just say they’ll have a front-row seat to their own death.”

Travis had sent the two men to Pompeii August 24th 79 A.D. The day Mt. Vesuvius erupted, burying the land in lava within 12 hrs. The mere thought of them there now made Travis burst out into giddy laughter.

The interrogator slammed him back. “Take him to his cell! Sensory deprivation until he begs!” That was the part Travis wanted to hear. Sensory deprivation. He knew if he made them mad enough, that would be the order. It was always the order. Usually, it meant hours or days of solitude and confusion. Today it meant privacy and a chance at rescue. If the programing worked and someone...somewhere...sometime figured it out. Two very big ‘if’s.’

They dragged Travis down the hall. He didn’t resist. A smile on his face the whole way, laughing maniacally. A smile that remained even as he was hurled into the far wall of his shallow cell.

The doors closed, the steel panels came down, and all was dark. He was alone. Just as planned.

In the pitch-black cell, stripped of sound and light, Travis sat cross-legged on the floor facing the far wall he had just been slammed into. Slowly, his laughter began to fade.

He pressed his forehead to the wall, whispering to no one, “Any minute now.”

## Chapter 25: Collision Course

**2183**

The rebel search party had barely cleared the base entrance when the DTO squad, already waiting in the shadows, with rifles raised, began to fire. The first volley shredded the night, muzzle flashes lighting up the pines.

The forest erupted in war.

A rebel's chest burst open, flinging him backward into the dirt. Another went down screaming, his leg nearly severed by automatic fire.

"CONTACT!" someone shouted, but it was already chaos.

The rebels scattered, trying to flank, but the DTO soldiers moved with surgical precision, armor glinting, and their formation tight. One rebel got off a clean shot, dropping a DTO soldier with a bullet through the throat. Another DTO soldier took a round to the head, helmet splitting in a spray of red mist.

But the cost was brutal. Four of the rebels lay dead in seconds, their blood soaking into the roots.

Inside the hidden entrance, everyone heard the exchange—each crack of gunfire reverberating down into the stone corridors. Alarms blared.

"They've found us," Keene muttered, face pale.

L's eyes narrowed. "Then it's now or never."

Alex's throat was dry, but he forced a crooked smile. "What's the worst that happens? If I'm right we find Travis, if I'm wrong, well the universe collapses but at least the soldiers won't be a problem anymore."

Keene actually chuckled, though it seemed strained. "Dark optimism. I like it."

Two rebels at opposite ends of the chamber hefted goggles. They synchronized them, portals shimmering into existence five feet in front of each operator. The blue ovals rippled, humming louder than usual.

"Start walking them in," L ordered.

The rebels obeyed, each step bringing the portals closer together.

Outside, the battle raged on.

One DTO soldier caught a round in the neck and dropped, thrashing. Another rebel went down clutching his abdomen, blood gushing between his fingers.

"Fall back!" one of the last two standing rebels yelled, dragging one of his wounded comrades back towards the entrance. Gunfire shredded bark all around them, bullets chewing the trees to splinters.

He hauled the bleeding man inside while his cover took down one more DTO soldier with a shot to the eye just as the reinforced stone door slammed shut.

The two DTO survivors pressed forward, firing until the entrance sealed. They paused, catching breath, their armor steaming from exertion.

The squad leader's face was a mask of fury. "Back to camp. We'll regroup and come back with the others once we have a plan of attack."

Inside, the portals were now just feet apart. "Closer!" L barked, her knuckles white on the console. "If Alex is correct, we should get an error code any minute now."

Sparks snapped between them, like lightning leaping from cloud to cloud. The hum grew to a deafening roar, rattling the stone walls.

The rebels reluctantly continued forward, bringing the portals closer together. All of a sudden, each felt a pull as if the portals themselves had become magnetic.

**2027**

In the sensory deprivation of his cell, Travis sat in the darkness, forehead against the wall. His breath came slow, measured.

Then—snap.

A spark arced across the stone. Then another. Tiny flares of blue danced before his eyes.

Travis's smile widened. "Well," he whispered, "took you long enough."

**2183**

The two portals began to pull stronger towards each other. "Commander L, still no error code and the pull is getting stronger. Perhaps we should abort." Too late. The magnetism between the portals began to drag the two together.

The two portals collided. Slamming together, drawn by an unseen force. And yet, still no error code. Instead, the two portals merged in a blinding flash, exploding outward into a single, massive vortex. The room howled with energy, hair whipping, papers flying.

Then—something fell out.

A body, ragged and battered, hitting the floor hard.

The vortex collapsed, leaving only silence and the acrid scent of ozone.

Everyone in the room froze, staring.

The man on the floor stirred, bloodied and gaunt, chains still hanging from his wrists. More affected by his first travel through time than most due to his weakened condition from months of abuse. He lifted his head with the last of his strength.

"I sure hope," he croaked, voice cracked, "y'all are the good guys."

Then he passed out cold.

Travis Calder was finally free.

## Chapter 26: Fractures

**79 A.D.**

Two DTO agents screamed as the mountain split open. Fire roared into the sky, a black column of ash blotting out the sun.

Lava surged down the streets of Pompeii, swallowing buildings. People fled in every direction, choking on ash, their skin blistering from the rain of molten rock.

One agent dropped his weapon, frozen in horror. “What is this place?!”

The other grabbed him, coughing, eyes wide with terror. “We’re in hell.”

The sky cracked as the eruption consumed them.

Travis’s brand of justice. Served.

**2027.**

The guards turned pale as they opened Travis’s cell. The cot was untouched. The bucket sat in its corner. Nothing was missing but Travis and his shackles.

"What the hell..." one guard whispered, his voice shaking. "Prisoner is gone. There's no sign of escape. Nothing."

The commander stormed in, staring at the walls, then at the ceiling. "Search the compound. Every room. Every vent. Every tunnel."

But deep down, they knew: Travis Calder was already gone.

**2042.**

The Superior sat in his chamber, bathed in the glow of flickering monitors.

Every screen carried breaking news. Hurricanes slamming coastlines. Earthquakes swallowing cities. Floods sweeping across farmland. Tornadoes in places they had never struck before.

Reporters spoke in frantic tones about how weather systems no longer followed predictable patterns, about oceans warming overnight, about fires that burned with no end.

The Superior leaned forward, sweat beading up on his forehead. His own present was... shifting.

History was rewriting itself.

And he was losing control.

**2215.**

The citadel trembled. Hairline cracks spiderwebbed across its foundations, shaking loose dust and stone. Sirens wailed as lights flickered.

The Masters stood in the central chamber, cloaked and grim.

"The fractures are accelerating," one rasped.

"Too much has changed in the past. Stability is failing," another replied.

A third hissed, "Then we send another team. Someone who can locate the breach and excise it."

"And if the damage cannot be undone?"

The chamber fell silent, the only sound was the groaning of their shifting citadel.

**2183. DTO Soldier Camp**

The remaining DTO squad returned to camp, dragging mud and blood with them.

Tricia sat tied to a post, her face streaked with tears. She shook her head violently as the squad leader approached, pistol in hand and anger in his eyes.

“You gave us what we needed,” he said flatly. “You’re no longer useful.”

“No… no, please,” Tricia sobbed, thrashing in her bonds. “Don’t—”

The gun fired. Her body slumped, lifeless.

Just then, the recon men returning from their mission of observation emerged from the trees. One of them adjusted his helmet. He glanced around for the missing soldiers then the scene at camp, expression blank. A dead girl and only half his team unaccounted for.

“What did we miss?”

**2183. Rebel Base Infirmary.**

Beeping monitors. White sheets.

Travis stirred awake, eyes fluttering. The sterile light burned his vision until a familiar face swam into view.

Dr. Keene.

Her hair was gray now. Deep lines creased her face. She looked decades older than when he'd last seen her months ago.

"Dr. Keene?" he rasped, voice weak. "You... you look..."

She gave a sad smile. "Old...You can say it. While it's only been months for you since you were taken, it's been many years for me, Travis."

He tried to sit up, groaning in pain. "What happened? Where am I?"

A voice spoke from the shadows.

"You're safe—for now."

Travis turned his head. A woman stepped forward. Older, sharp-eyed, but with a strange warmth behind the steel.

It was L.

She told him everything—the students, the rebels, the battle with the DTO, the fractures in time itself.

Travis listened in silence, hands trembling, eyes darting between Keene and L.

Something about L gnawed at him. The cadence of her voice. The curve of her jaw. She reminded him of someone—his grandmother, maybe? But he forced the thought away.

Finally, his voice cracked. "If what you say is true... then all of this—" He looked down at the scars from his captivity. "—is my fault."

L tilted her head, waiting.

Travis clenched his fists. "If I've put all of humanity in danger, then I have to help fix my mistakes. What's the plan?"

The monitors beeped, the room heavy with the weight of his words.

Finally, L sighed. Her voice became heavy with despair as she said, "Everything we've tried to combat the DTO has failed and resulted in many casualties. We lost contact with every other rebel base years ago. Our only plan since, has been to survive until we could locate and rescue you. As far as we know, we're the last of the resistance and now they know where we are."

Travis sat up.

"Then we need to get everyone out of here until we can come up with a plan." He said with a sense of urgency.

Keene asked, "Where can we possibly go that the DTO wouldn't find us?"

Travis smiled. "You mean *when* can we go?"

He looked down at the I.V.

Then back up at Keene. "Can someone unhook this stuff?"

To Be Continued...

For part two of Travis Calder's adventure or other books please visit:

www.qftgames.com or https://books.by/app/bookstores/qft

Please direct any questions, concerns, or suggestions about what you have read to J. Leon at qftgamesllc@gmail.com

Thank you so much for reading the first part of my story!

www.QFTgames.com

May God bless you and your family...

Printed in Dunstable, United Kingdom

79100151R00109